What Others Are Saying

"*A Journey of Hope* is a true story that conveys the full aspect of knowing Christ through the unexpected ups and downs of life. Reading this story will bring insight to anyone walking through joy and pain. It will strengthen the reader as they identify with this journey filled with hope and victory in Christ."

— Dr. Jim Burkett
Director, Oklahoma School of
Apologetics and Practical Theology
Tulsa, Oklahoma

"This book will captivate the hearts of those who read it and will bring value, practicality, clarity, and meaning to the life experiences we all encounter. The love, grace and charm with which they share their story will leave you with a deeper abiding faith in Jesus."

—Pa:

D1212002

"This book tells the story—and tells it well—of a family's journey of faith. Through good times and difficult seasons, their consistent reliance on God is an example for us to follow. You will be encouraged by this book."

—Dr. Don McMinn
Associate Pastor
Stonebriar Community Church
Frisco, Texas

A JOURNEY OF
HOPE

Jennifer Dunlap
Romans 15:13

Dyler & Elizabeth,
Love,
Cathie
Ps. 46:10-11

A JOURNEY OF
HOPE

EXPERIENCING THE HOPE OF CHRIST
IN TIMES OF JOY AND PAIN

JENNIFER GENTRY
WITH
CATHERINE WARE AND JOHN WARE

TATE PUBLISHING
AND ENTERPRISES, LLC

A Journey of Hope
Copyright © 2016 by Jennifer Gentry. All rights reserved.

No part of this publication may be reproduced, stored in a retrieval system or transmitted in any way by any means, electronic, mechanical, photocopy, recording or otherwise without the prior permission of the author except as provided by USA copyright law.

Scripture quotations marked (ESV) are from *The Holy Bible, English Standard Version*®, copyright © 2001 by Crossway Bibles, a publishing ministry of Good News Publishers. Used by permission. All rights reserved.

Scripture quotations marked (KJV) are taken from the *Holy Bible, King James Version*, Cambridge, 1769. Used by permission. All rights reserved.

Scripture quotations marked (MSG) are taken from *The Message*. Copyright © 1993, 1994, 1995, 1996, 2000, 2001, 2002. Used by permission of NavPress Publishing Group.

Scripture quotations marked (NIV) are taken from the *Holy Bible, New International Version*®, NIV®. Copyright © 1973, 1978, 1984 by Biblica, Inc.™ Used by permission of Zondervan. All rights reserved worldwide. www.zondervan.com

Scripture quotations marked (NKJV) are taken from the *New King James Version*. Copyright © 1982 by Thomas Nelson, Inc. Used by permission. All rights reserved.

Scripture quotations marked (NLT) are taken from the *Holy Bible, New Living Translation*, copyright © 1996. Used by permission of Tyndale House Publishers, Inc., Wheaton, Illinois 60189. All rights reserved.

This book is designed to provide accurate and authoritative information with regard to the subject matter covered. This information is given with the understanding that neither the author nor Tate Publishing, LLC is engaged in rendering legal, professional advice. Since the details of your situation are fact dependent, you should additionally seek the services of a competent professional.

The opinions expressed by the author are not necessarily those of Tate Publishing, LLC.

Published by Tate Publishing & Enterprises, LLC
127 E. Trade Center Terrace | Mustang, Oklahoma 73064 USA
1.888.361.9473 | www.tatepublishing.com

Tate Publishing is committed to excellence in the publishing industry. The company reflects the philosophy established by the founders, based on Psalm 68:11,
"The Lord gave the word and great was the company of those who published it."

Book design copyright © 2016 by Tate Publishing, LLC. All rights reserved.
Cover design by Norlan Balazo
Interior design by Mary Jean Archival

Published in the United States of America

ISBN: 978-1-68270-788-3
1. Religion / Christian Life / Spiritual Growth
2. Religion / Christian Ministry / Counseling & Recovery
16.08.13

Contents

Part II

Part III

Acknowledgments

A SPECIAL THANK-YOU goes to my talented and gifted friend Camille Waage. Your belief in this project, your mentorship, and divine ability to paint beautiful word pictures brings life to these pages. Your commitment to me and to this book has helped make this God-sized vision a reality.

Foreword

HAVE YOU EVER wondered in the midst of uncertainty why God allowed you to experience certain things? Do you ever doubt His presence and care for you? What do you do when you feel all alone and unsure of what the future brings? Join us as we meditate on God's Word, ask Father questions, and reflect on a significant journey He chose for us to take as a young family. As Jennifer, John, and I share our stories, my personal prayer is that you will find hope and comfort in knowing our God is faithful, and He cares passionately about you! May He reveal His love and compassion for you as you read His Word, pray, and learn to listen to His still small voice.

He says, "Be still and know that I am God; I will be exalted among the nations, I will be exalted in the earth." The Lord Almighty is with us; the God of Jacob is our fortress (Psalm 46:10–11 NIV).

August 28, 2015
Catherine H. Ware

As a young husband and father, I came face-to-face with the trust issue. Simply stated:

"Will you, or will you not trust God, no matter what? Is He indeed trustworthy? Will you lead your family to trust God?" I decided that there is no other choice but to trust Him even when nothing makes sense. Life's journey is replete with twists, turns, bumps, jumps, sharp curves, and deep potholes. It also includes great heights, grand views, wonderful traveling companions, and amazing discoveries. For those who choose *the Way*, it includes a lifetime of divine direction. Through it all, I've discovered that trust in God is the only way to travel! Join our family as we share our story of discovering God's faithfulness. We pray that your trust level and intimacy with the living God will grow wider and deeper. Above all, we want to acknowledge His faithfulness and trustworthiness!

"Trust in the Lord with all your heart and lean not on your own understanding. In all your ways submit to Him and He will make your path straight" (Proverbs 3:5–6, ESV).

August 28, 2015
John A. Ware

Part I

The Phone Call

Let the peace of Christ rule in your hearts,
since as members of one body you were
called to peace. And be thankful.

—*Colossians 3:15*, NIV

John
March 26, 1972

MY HANDS GRIPPED the steering wheel as my mustard-yellow Ford Maverick flew down Interstate 30 at eighty miles per hour. The Dallas-Fort Worth Turnpike saw few cars on a Sunday night, and for this I was grateful. At work just minutes prior, I had received a phone call—*the* phone call. Cathie was headed to the hospital in labor with our firstborn.

I had been deep in production details of that evening's ten o'clock news. My job as a floor director was demanding, to say the least, in those hours prior to the scheduled news broadcast. While cameras were rolling, I was responsible for the placement of the cameras, newscasters, and everything else that happened down on the floor. To prepare for all of these details, the production director and I were marking the script for that evening's broadcast. When the call arrived, the floor exploded in a roar of whoops and applause. The first words out of my mouth were, "I don't know who's going to do this tonight, but I'm not. I'm gone. I'm headed for Fort Worth!" The production director, a father himself of six children, quickly jumped in with "Don't worry. We've got someone who will take it. Don't worry about it. You just drive carefully."

I suppose I tried to drive carefully as instructed by my well-meaning coworker. But I certainly didn't drive slowly. *You* try to keep your foot off the gas when the hospital is over forty miles away.

So, down the freeway, I sped as fast as that mustard-yellow car would take me, all the while saying repeatedly to myself, "Let the peace of Christ rule and be thankful. Let peace rule and be thankful. Let peace rule and be thankful!"

The Cure for Anxiety

Therefore I tell you, do not worry about your life,
what you will eat or drink; or about your body,
what you will wear. Is not life more than food,
and the body more than clothes? Can any one of
you by worrying add a single hour to your life?

—Matthew 6:25,27 NIV

Cathie
March 26, 1972

MY EYES WERE glued to the TV. Settled into the couch, lime sherbet in my lap and spoon in hand, I was an hour and a half into a gripping murder mystery. My heart raced and every muscle tensed as the main character rounded the corner. And then.

What? Water everywhere! On the couch, on my clothes—I couldn't stop it! What was happening? Wait, maybe it was, no! My due date was over a week away. This couldn't *really* be happening now, could it?

Throwing down my tub of sherbet, I grabbed the phone and dialed the numbers for my obstetrician. A woman's voice answered. "Hello?"

"Yes, is Dr. Turner there? This is Cathie Ware, one of his patients, and I think my water just broke. I think I need to go to the hospital."

"Well…he's at a party right now. Um…I'll do what I can to get word to him, but there is a chance that he might not make it."

A party? What was I going to do without my doctor? Frantically, I called my next-door neighbor, Julie, a close friend of mine. After hearing her promise that she would be right over, I hung up the phone and ran to my room to begin packing. *Lord! I'm not ready for this! My suitcase isn't packed, my husband is at work, and my doctor is at a party. How can I do this?* I crammed clothes into a suitcase while water continued to pool on the floor. Julie finally arrived and thrust a handful of Maxi Pads into my hand, grabbed the other, and said, "Come on, Cathie, we have to get to the hospital!"

Throwing a raincoat (yes, a *raincoat*) over my wet clothes, I ran out of the room, suitcase in hand. Right as I reached the front door, I stopped suddenly, *John has no idea this is happening!* I thought to myself.

"I have to call John!" I said to Julie. My hands shook as I dialed his work number. When I heard his voice on the other end, I almost cried. "It's time! I'm heading to the hospital. Meet me there!"

I received the news of my pregnancy in the summer of 1971. John and I were living in married student housing while I was finishing my undergraduate degree at Texas Wesleyan and John was studying for his master's degree at Southwestern Theological Seminary. The news was surprising. John described it as shocking. We were both feeling scared, ill-equipped, overwhelmed at the prospect of parenting. It just didn't seem to fit into our "plan." I was interviewed for jobs and finished my degree. John was deep into his theological studies while working at a TV station. We weren't ready to be parents! As a new Christian, I knew I could bring these worries to God, but I didn't know His Word well enough to find verses that would bring me comfort. So I sat down and just opened the Bible. The pages opened to Matthew chapter 6, and these words—the chapter heading for verses 25–27—seemed to lift right out of the onionskin pages.

"The Cure for Anxiety." I had not read these verses before, but the chapter heading inspired me to read on.

> "Therefore I tell you, do not worry about your life, what you will eat or drink: or about your body, what you will wear. Is not life more than food, and the body more than clothes? Can any one of you by worrying add a single hour to your life?"

People always say never to depend on this kind of roulette-style Bible reading, especially when trying to hear a specific message from the Lord. But those words in that moment seemed to come straight from the mouth of God: a message of comfort from a loving father to His frightened child, a reminder of His presence and plan for my life. He seemed to tell me *I'm going to take care of your little baby.*

Over the next few months, our shock gave way to joyful anticipation as we celebrated our news with friends and family. I was blessed with a baby shower in my honor and also attended several baby showers for close friends. John and I grew closer together as we spent hours planning and dreaming of our new life as parents.

Now, as I walked through the doors of the hospital, I saw a very excited and slightly shaken John. He had arrived before I did! We were also surprised to hear that several phone calls had been taken by the hospital receptionist. Friends were calling to see how we were doing. They had heard about our pending delivery on the evening news! The time had come. My husband and I, young and in love, unsure of the future but sure of the One who was guiding the way—we were about to become a family.

Labor and Delivery

Hear my voice when I call, Lord; be
merciful to me and answer me.

—*Psalm 27:7*, NIV

Cathie
March 26, 1972

MY EYELIDS BEGAN to flutter gently as my mind ebbed and
flowed in and out of a sleepy haze. Haunting sounds came to
me in echoing waves, long unfamiliar, desperate sounds that
were getting frighteningly louder. Sounds are all around me,
animal-like. In an instant, my peaceful slumber was consumed
by fear as my body jerked awake, and my eyes flew open in
terror. I was closed in on all sides by curtains that towered
over me like stone walls. There was screaming coming from
the other side of the curtain on my left, moaning on the right.
I tried to lift my arms to push myself up and found them tied
down, shackled. I was trapped, afraid, alone.

As my eyes tried to take in my surroundings, I saw my swollen belly under the sheets. Hospital. Baby. My terrified heart leaped suddenly with joy at this familiar recognition. I'm going to have a baby today! But where am I? Why am I restrained in this unfamiliar bed? Who are these women suffering so terribly on the other side of the curtains?

As my mind tried to process the terrifying scene, I began to put the pieces together. I remembered arriving at the hospital with my dear friend, dressed in that silly raincoat, hoping that the slick waterproof fabric would hide the mess I was making, which, embarrassingly, it did not. Ever since we had left my apartment, I was feeling a low, tight ache in my belly every ten to fifteen minutes or so. It was certainly not the stomach-grabbing contractions I saw played out on TV, but I knew the time had to be near. My water had already broken for heaven's sake! This baby was coming *soon*!

After the check-in process was done, I was led to a prelabor room, where I changed into a hospital gown and tried to get comfortable in the provided hospital bed.

Expressionless medical staff came in and out of the room, hardly talking to me at all, prepping me for my upcoming labor and delivery. I lay there, surrounded by people but feeling completely alone in that room, needing to be comforted, longing to be nurtured.

When the nameless people left, I was even more alone. When the door opened and I saw my dear husband's face peeking through, I almost cried out of the flood of emotions that blanketed me in that moment—joy, relief, excitement, fear. It was almost too much. John came straight to my side, spoke to me reassuringly, and helped me breathe through my next contraction, but then he had to leave. Oh, how I wished we had been able to make time for him to take that birth preparation class! I needed him to stay with me and was devastated when he had to leave. I was once again alone in that sterile prep room, my eyes welling up with fearful tears, riding out each contraction as they strengthened and became more painful with each wave.

I don't think I can make it! I thought to myself as a strong contraction gripped my body and caused me to feel faint. The contractions were coming faster now, and I was still alone, trying to remember my breathing exercises, trying to survive the intensity of each painful squeeze. I prayed aloud, "God, help me!"

Four hours had passed, they told me, but it felt like four days. "Only five cm dilated," the nurse said, and my entire body tensed with the frustration, exhaustion, and ever-increasing pain. I had wanted so badly to labor and deliver without using any medication, but as each contraction took over with its unrelenting, painful pressure, my mind fought for sanity, and every part of my body longed for relief. When my doctor came in, I begged for something to help me sleep. I wanted to be an active participant in the actual birthing process, but my exhausted body screamed for some rest and relief. I knew I could survive this if I could just get a little bit of sleep. I longed again for John to be there with me. I desperately wanted him to hold my hands as they clenched again in an effort to push back the pain that seemed to completely consume me.

The next person to enter the room was the anesthesiologist. He explained that the medicine that would drip into my IV would soon allow me to fall asleep, and I immediately felt my body relax in anticipation of sweet relief. Another contraction pulled and wrenched, but I could already feel my body feeling heavy on the hospital bed. My thoughts went once again to my husband, and then darkness took over.

—⚬—

It was from this medication-induced sleep that I awoke into that nightmare that was called the active labor room. In that moment of fear, I began to think even more terrifying thoughts: *What else did they do to me while I was asleep? Did anyone see me in an embarrassing position? What is happening to me?*

Another nameless nurse walked by my bed—it was actually more of a table—and I called out to her, "I can hear women screaming. I don't like this!"

"Sorry, miss. You're going to have to get over it. This is the active labor room, and you are in active labor."

"But I have to go to the bathroom! I need help—please, help me!"

"You're just going to have to do it on the table."

And to my horror, she walked away. No help, no comfort, no understanding of my fears and potential embarrassment. I felt victimized and degraded. Once again, a wave of despair and sadness flooded over me, which then brought a sudden feeling of anger. This was supposed to be the happiest day of my life! Instead of my arms holding a precious newborn, they were shackled to an uncomfortable hospital bed. Instead of rejoicing alongside my loving husband, I was surrounded by agonizing screams.

I realized right then that I needed to talk to my doctor, *now*. I called for a nurse and demanded that he be called. Just moments later, I saw his concerned face appear in the doorway.

"Please get me out of here," I implored weakly.

His understanding eyes looked right into mine. "You've got it," he said.

The delivery room was sterile and medical, but it was a welcome relief to be tended to by kind nurses. The epidural that I had requested after leaving the active labor room had numbed me from the waist down, so I was only feeling pressure. No pain. And my wonderful doctor was there, coaching me through this final stage.

Excitement filled every cell of my body as I realized, *This is really going to happen!* I heard my doctor say, "I see the head!" And I prepared my body for the final push to bring my child into the world. I thought about the names John and I had lovingly chosen: John Mark for a boy and Jennifer for a girl. No middle names yet, but we had prayed over those first names, and I couldn't wait to call our little one by his or her precious name. Suddenly, I heard my doctor say, "She has to be a girl because she's coming through and her little fist is like this." He held his clenched fist against his cheek, and I smiled at the thought of those tiny fingers. With one final push, I heard him shout, "It's a girl! It's a girl!"

Held in the air by my doctor's strong hands was my beautiful daughter. All pink with curly dark hair crowning that perfect head, she was the most beautiful baby I had ever seen in my entire life. She was wailing and wailing, letting the whole world know she was here. But I thought it looked like she was smiling at the same time. Perfect. Miraculous. *Mine*.

My daughter.

My beautiful Jennifer.

Delivery Room

Come unto me, all ye that labour and are
heavy laden, and I will give you rest.

—Matthew 11:28, KJV

John
March 26, 1972

DELIVERY ROOM. I had read this plastic placard on the cold metal door about a hundred times. I was pacing, pacing, pacing, sitting, can't sit, pacing again. Every time I passed the door, I read those words and wondered what was happening on the other side. Every time I sat down, I looked up and saw those words staring me down. Sometimes, they seemed to taunt me.

Why hadn't I just gone to that childbirth class? I knew that my work schedule hadn't allowed it. I knew there was just no way to attend the classes with Cathie when I had a forty-five-mile commute, a nonflexible TV broadcast schedule, and a limited childbirth class schedule. But in this moment—this harrowing, nail-biting, hair-pulling moment—I was filled with frustration and regret. I wanted to push past those heavy metal doors and stand next to my wife, hold her hand, and brush her hair away from her face. I wanted to be a sweet familiar comfort to her in a sea of strange faces. I wanted to cheer her on and be with her as we together would watch our firstborn come into the world.

But my hands didn't hold a childbirth class completion certificate. And that was the only all-access pass to the delivery room.

So I had to wait in the hallway outside the delivery room. Oh, how I had to wait.

Emotions and thoughts over the past nine months all came flooding back into my present awareness as I paced and waited. Those past several months had been what I liked to call a gestation of parental preparation—mentally, emotionally, and spiritually. As I pressed into the Lord and sought Him for answers, my original cry of "Lord, I'm not ready to be a dad!" was beautifully transformed into "How can I best prepare my home to raise a child to know and love You?"

And He had answered. Those original thoughts of inadequacy and fear had eventually given way to excitement and purpose. I was ready. But now I had to wait. Just when I thought I might burst from the nervous energy buzzing through every fiber of my being, the plastic Delivery Room placard started to move. The metal door swung open, and I caught a glimpse of green scrubs. I saw my beautiful wife lying on a metal gurney being wheeled toward me, and in her arms was a little bundle wrapped in a light blue blanket. Through his mask, the doctor announced, "Congratulations, it's a girl!" I rushed to Cathie's side, and the attendant stopped so that I could see our new little one. Gently pulling back the blanket, I saw the most beautiful face looking back at me. Eyes tentatively blinking, nose wrinkling, perfect rosebud mouth. I wanted to say something, wanted to shout out in exuberant joy, but the sounds and syllables stuck like glue to the back of my throat. I was speechless. It was love at first sight. Cathie looked up and gently said to me, "I'd like to introduce you to Jennifer Michelle."

My Girl, God's Gift

Children are a gift from the Lord, they are a
reward from Him. Children born to a young
man are like arrows in a warrior's hands.

—Psalm 127:3,4, NLT

Cathie
March 27, 1972

"Is she really mine?"

The emotion welled up within me with such force that
my eyes pricked with tears, and then I felt the warmth trickle
down my cheeks. That wriggly body, full of life, full of energy,
kicking and wailing, letting the whole world know that she
had arrived—she was *mine*.

The nurses were bustling about weighing her, measuring
her, and I couldn't take my eyes off those tiny toes and that
curly hair. I wanted to remember every moment, mental
snapshots of a day I knew I would never forget.

I was overwhelmed by love for this precious little girl who was being carefully wrapped in a soft blue blanket. It was an incredible, instantaneous love—something I had never experienced.

Then suddenly, I had the distinct understanding that Jennifer was not truly mine. She was a gift. She didn't belong to me like something I would possess, but rather, she was on loan to me from the Lord. She belonged to *Him*, and I was being given the awesome responsibility of caring for someone so special to our Creator.

As I was considering that sobering thought, filled with gratitude, a nurse gently handed me my tiny baby. As the weight of her perfect head settled into the crook of my elbow, I saw the soft edge of the blue blanket barely brush her soft pink cheek. It took my breath away.

What a miraculous gift, I thought in wonder of all that had happened, all that had changed in me instantly in that moment. Looking down at that beautiful face, I knew that life would never be the same. God had called me to be a mother to this precious little girl. It was the most amazing gift I had ever received.

First Year

Trust in the Lord with all your heart and lean not
on your own understanding; in all your ways submit
to Him, and He will make your paths straight.

—Proverbs 3:5–6, NIV

Cathie
June 1972

"Jennifer hasn't gained as much weight as I'd like to see. I recommend that you begin feeding her formula."

The pediatrician's words and concerned look worried me. I was a new mother with so many questions. I thought back to the first week checkup, when the doctor mentioned a possible issue with weight gain. I didn't worry much at the time. She was a little peanut to start with—only about six and a half pounds—and all of her other development seemed normal. She was a happy, busy, easy baby. So flexible without a real need for a strict schedule. This fit our lives perfectly. As young leaders in our church, we were always out and about, and our life as a couple easily transitioned to a family of three with such a content baby. She played happily, napped anywhere, and charmed everyone everywhere we went. But now, sitting here in the cold sterile pediatrician's office, the warm happy bundle in my lap couldn't keep the chill off my spine. Was something wrong with my milk? Was I not feeding her long enough? I didn't want to even consider anything more serious. I had so many questions, typical for a new mother, but the only answer, my only pediatrician-recommended option, seemed to be to abandon the ease of breast-feeding and try formula.

And what a disaster that was! Poor little thing reacted horribly to the awful-smelling stuff. The little she kept down made another kind of mess hours later. A milk allergy was suspected, so we switched to a much more expensive soy formula. This seemed to ease some of her symptoms, but not all. I was so relieved when we were able to introduce other kinds of foods, but even those did not completely clear up her tummy troubles.

I tried not to worry about the slow weight gain. I tried not to think about the concern I saw on that doctor's face. All the while, Jennifer continued to be the happy active baby that she was from the very beginning. Over the next few months, my concerns faded as we delighted in the first year's milestones—rolling over, first attempts to crawl, first hesitant steps. Our sweet happy baby was becoming a toddler before our eyes, and we were enjoying the blessings of our family of three.

Florida

Hear my cry, O God; attend unto my prayer. From
the end of the earth will I cry unto thee, when
my heart is overwhelmed: lead me to the rock
that is higher than I. For thou hast been a shelter
for me, and a strong tower from the enemy.

—Psalm 61:1–3, KJV

John
August 1973

"WE'RE MOVING TO Florida!"

My master's degree was completed, and I had received a
call to pastor a youth group in Florida. Jennifer was a happy
sixteen-month-old toddler and, despite her continuing food
issues, was delighting us daily with new discoveries, a budding
awareness of language, and an ever-present smile.

We settled into our new home and immediately immersed
ourselves in our new ministry. Jennifer was always with us.

As Cathie rode her bicycle all over the charming beach community, Jennifer rode along with her perched, grinning in her little bucket seat mounted to the back. She became a mascot of sorts in our youth group, her feet hardly touched the floor as she was passed from teenager to teenager. At retreats, youth events, all-night lock-ins, she joined us for all of it and loved every minute of it.

Then one evening in November, Jennifer didn't seem herself. "I think she might be running a fever," Cathie said with a worried tone. The thermometer confirmed it: 102 degrees. We hoped it was something "normal" for toddlers: a mild virus, a new tooth. But when the days went by and the fevers continued, along with the ongoing problems with weight gain and other gastrointestinal issues, we knew we needed to see our pediatrician.

The first time I heard the words *kidney reflux*—words with which we would become all too familiar—Cathie and I were seated side by side in the pediatrician's office with Jennifer on Cathie's lap. A urinalysis had revealed bacteria in the sample, and further testing would be needed.

"What kinds of testing?" I asked.

"We will start with some blood tests and may need to do an x-ray, depending on what we find."

I looked at my sweet, innocent toddler completely unaware of what was in her very near future. I prayed that the pain would be minimal, that our questions would be answered, and that her healing would be quick and complete.

News

But seek first His kingdom and His righteousness, and all these things will be given to you as well. Therefore do not worry about tomorrow, for tomorrow will worry about itself. Each day has enough trouble of its own.

—*Matthew 6:33–34*, NIV

Cathie
Fall 1973

"Let's have some tests run."

The doctor was calm as he spoke these words, but my heart was fearful. My mind was racing with the questions, possibilities, unknowns. What kind of tests? Would Jennifer be in pain? Would her issues finally be relieved?

"But seek first His kingdom." What a comforting reminder! It wasn't about what was ahead, but *Who* was ahead of us. If I kept that in the forefront of my thoughts, I didn't have to fear. One of the early tests revealed a UTI, and we brought home the first of what would be many medications for our pigtailed little girl. Thankfully, this one tasted good and went down easy.

"And all these things will be given to you as well." Oh how true this was and is in our lives. We were immeasurably blessed by the support of our church family. They truly carried us through some very difficult days. After moving to a new city, our new church surrounded us and embraced us.

Jennie was everyone's baby, and she thrived on all of the love and attention. People energized her. Even when she was not feeling well, she always lit up when we entered a room full of people. She especially loved spending time with her dad in youth ministry. If everyone was singing, she wanted to be right up front. During teaching times, there were no shortage of laps for her to sit on. At summer swimming parties, she had to be right in the center of the pool.

Loved, supported, blessed, my heart was filled to overflowing by "all these things"—all of these precious godly people pouring themselves into our new little family.

Pink

Love must be sincere. Hate what is evil; cling to what is good. Be devoted to one another in love. Honor one another above yourselves. Never be lacking in zeal, but keep your spiritual fervor, serving the Lord. Be joyful in hope, patient in affliction, faithful in prayer. Share with the Lord's people who are in need. Practice hospitality.

—*Romans 12:9–13*, NIV

Jennie (three years old)
Spring 1975

PINK! I *LOVE* pink! And I like this medicine. It tastes yummy, like bananas; not yucky, like cough syrup. And it's pink—my favorite color! Mommy lets me have the pink medicine at breakfast *and* before bed, so I must be pretty special.

I also feel special when we go to church and Mommy and Daddy's friends smile at me and talk to me. I have *so many* grammas and grampas and aunties and uncles, and well, they're not really my grammas and grampas and aunties and uncles, but they sure love me, and they love my mommy and daddy too.

I'm glad I feel so much love because sometimes my body doesn't feel good. I get cold and then hot, and I just want to sit with Mommy and rock for a while. And I don't like to go potty like a big girl. Mommy and Daddy are so happy when I do, but it feels yucky, and I don't like it. And I have to go a lot. I don't know why I have to go a lot, but the doctor says that I have to. The doctor lives at the hospital. We went yesterday, and everything was so *big*. There was silver everywhere, and I lay down on a silver table. It was cold—*really cold*—not soft and warm like my bed at home. There were people in the room, but not Mommy. The doctor showed me a big black mask and put it on my nose and mouth. He told me to blow into it like a balloon. I *love* balloons! That made me smile. *It's okay, Mommy. I'm not scared. I get to blow into a balloon! I love you, Mommy. I love balloons, and I love pink!*

Melodies, Memory Verses, and Medicine

"A cheerful heart is good medicine, but a crushed spirit dries up the bones.

—*Proverbs 17:22*, NIV

Cathie
Summer 1975

"Up on the counter, sweetie! It's time to take your medicine." I said these words in a cheerful singsong way that brought Jennie into the kitchen with a smile.

"Is it the pink kind?" Jennie asked excitedly.

"Sure is!" I said and lifted her up to sit on the edge of the counter. As I opened the cabinet door, I scanned the Bible verses written on a piece of paper taped to the inside of the door: "He took up our infirmities and bore our diseases" (Matthew 8:17b), "For I am the Lord who heals you" (Exodus

15:26b), "Praise the Lord, my soul, and forget not all His benefits–who forgives all your sins and heals all your diseases" (Psalm 103:2–3).

Verse after verse spoke comfort in that moment as I reached for the bottle of medicine. Today, I chose Jennie's favorite verse, and we said it together as I poured the pink liquid into the spoon.

"A merry heart does good…" I began.

"Like medicine!" Jennie finished. She paused and grinned and then opened her mouth wide to take the spoonful of syrupy liquid. She swallowed hard, and her little voice asked expectantly, "Can we sing the song too?"

"Only if you help me sing it!" I said, and we began to sing together:

> A merry heart doeth good like a medicine,
> Like a medicine is a merry heart;
> But a broken spirit drieth up the bones.
> But a merry heart is a joy to the Lord.

What beauty and joy came from that little voice. As those little legs dangled over the edge of the counter, she sang and smiled and sang some more. In that moment, it was hard to even believe that pain was a part of her life. It seemed silly to think that a shelf full of medicine was even needed. How could a little girl who faces daily discomfort experience such delight?

But the medicine was daily reality, just as God's Word was a daily joy. And I knew that if I could put confidence in doctors to prescribe the right medicine to protect Jennie's body from further infection, I could trust even more my loving Heavenly Father to protect and provide comfort and healing, both for my little girl's body, and for a momma's heart. *Dear Lord, please don't ever let this joy depart from my little Jennie. Thank you for your sweet Word that gives us peace in the midst of pain. Thank you for your goodness. Thank you for your healing power.*

Songs and Stripes

But He was pierced for our transgressions, He
was crushed for our iniquities; the punishment
that brought us peace was on Him, and by
His wounds [stripes, KJV] we are healed.

—*Isaiah 53:5*, NIV

Jennie (three years old)
Summer 1975

"MEDICINE TIME!"

I love medicine time because it's also singing time! Today, Mommy and I sang my *favorite* song called "A Merry Heart Doeth Good like a Medicine." I like all the songs we sing, but that one is my favorite.

Also "The Joy of the Lord is my Strength" is my other favorite. I like the words "He fills my heart with laughter" because my mommy smiles so big, and it makes me smile too.

I also get to sit up high on the counter, just high enough to look at Mommy's pretty face as we sing songs together. And we pray too. It is so fun!

Yesterday, my mommy said a verse from the Bible. It was about Jesus's stripes and being healed. At first, I was confused. Stripes? On Jesus? Like on pink ribbon candy? That's just silly! But then Mommy said that those stripes were very special. That they were scratches on Jesus, kind of like the scratch on my knee from falling on the sidewalk. But Jesus was hurt much worse. Really, *really* hurt. She told me that He was hurt so bad that He died, and that made me sad. But then she said that Jesus's hurt would take my pain, and that I could be *healed!* She said that He wasn't dead anymore but was alive and wanted to be my friend! She looked right at me and said, "This is something we believe."

And, you know what? I think I believe it too!

Questioning and Comfort

Praise be to the God and Father of our Lord Jesus
Christ, the Father of compassion and the God of
all comfort who comforts us in all our troubles,
so that we can comfort those in any trouble with
the comfort we ourselves receive from God.

—2 Corinthians 1:3–4, NIV

Perfume and incense bring joy to the
heart, and the pleasantness of a friend
springs from their heartfelt advice.

—Proverbs 27:9, NIV

Cathie
Fall 1975

HOW LONG, O Lord? How long will this last? I lost count of the
number of times I cried this prayer out to God. Each time I
had to leave little Jennie in a cold x-ray room, every time I

looked into her eyes welling up with tears from the pain, in those moments of doubt, questions, even despair, I asked the question again: "How long?"

I wanted it to be over. I longed for a day that did not call for medicine and hospital visits. I prayed for relief for my little girl. How long? These doubts plagued me as I wrestled with my unbelief. I was a pastor's wife, for heaven's sake! I wasn't supposed to struggle with these kinds of questions.

Sitting across the kitchen table from a dear sister in Christ, coffee cup in hand, I shared these questions, these doubts. With tears in my eyes, I told her that I felt that God had turned His back on me. That He didn't see me in my despair. That He didn't notice the pain in Jennie's eyes.

"Oh, Cathie, He will never turn His back on you. He loves you. He's there for you, and He's going to come through for you." And like a warm beam of sunlight, I felt relief and comfort wash over me as the truth of her words sank deep in my soul. In my head, I always knew that this was true, but it had to penetrate into the darkest areas of my heart to a place that was carefully guarded because letting it go would be risky. Letting go would be relinquishing all control. But in the moment, with my coffee cup resting in the palm of my hand, I understood that letting go was freedom. Freedom to trust. Freedom to believe. Freedom to love. Her words allowed those unbelieving corners of my heart to soften and to truly trust in our Great Physician.

Oh, Lord. Thank you for your provision of this dear friend. Thank you for surrounding our family with other believers who can speak the truth of your words into our hearts. May I be a comfort to others as I have been comforted today, Amen.

Tabby

A friend loves at all times and a brother
is born for a time of adversity.

—Proverbs 17:17, NIV

Jennie (three years old)
Summer 1975

"JENNIE! JENNIE! CAN you play?"

"Please, Mommy? Can I play with Tabby today? Yes? Oh boy!"

The door is too heavy, but Mommy can open it for me, and there is my best friend in the world, Tabby! She is running so fast. Well, not as fast as other kids, but fast enough! She is waving her arms so that I can see her.

"I see you, Tabby! Mommy said we can play! Wanna make mud pies again today?"

My backyard is our special place, our imaginary world. It is fun, and it is safe. And we are best friends. Best friends laugh and play house and make mud pies. And that's what we will do today.

Tabby doesn't care that I hurt inside sometimes because she hurts outside sometimes. Her legs hurt and don't work right. That's why she isn't so fast. But she still runs good, at least I think so. And she doesn't care that I have to take lots of medicine. I love her so much, and she loves me. I'm so glad that she is my best friend.

"Tabby! Your mud pies look delicious."

Friends
(Disabilities and Discoveries)

Christ arrives right on time to make this happen. He
didn't, and doesn't, wait for us to get ready. He presented
himself for the sacrificial death when we were far too
weak and rebellious to do anything to get ourselves
ready. And even if we hadn't been so weak, we wouldn't
have known what to do anyway. We can understand
someone dying for a person worth dying for, and we
can understand how someone good and noble could
inspire us to selfless sacrifice. But God put His love
on the line for us by offering His Son in sacrificial
death while we were of no use whatever to Him.

—*Romans 5:6–8*, MSG

Cathie
Summer 1975

"Jennie!"

I heard the sweet voice of our neighbor call out from across the street, and I knew what the next question would be...

"Please, Mommy, can I play with Tabby today?"

As I smiled and nodded my head, I saw Jennie's face light up like I'd seen it light up so many times before at the thought of playing with her special friend, Tabby. What a pair those two were! They had a special bond that no one could understand. I'm not sure that they even fully understood the disabilities that so tightly connected their hearts and spirits.

Tabby was born with a birth defect that caused one leg to be shorter than the other. She was an amazing little girl—brave, resilient, confident. A tiny little thing with a giant heart. And she loved my Jennie. It was an almost daily tradition opening the door for Jennie to meet her friend, and watching Tabby run toward her as fast as she could, despite her slight hobble, with her waving arms outstretched, and her voice calling Jennie's name.

I was comforted by God's provision of friendship for these two girls, each with their own disability: Tabby's external and Jennie's internal. Both understood grown-up words like *medical procedures* and *prescriptions*, yet both delighted in childlike play, making mud pies and playing house. And both shared an understanding that they were a little different than other kids, but that they had each other. Kindred hearts, those two.

I was also deeply moved to see a picture of my relationship with my loving Savior in the unbridled exuberance of little Tabby running to greet Jennie, her best friend in the world. With tears in my eyes, I realized at that moment that I can come to Jesus in any way. I can run to Him, carrying with me all my ailments, my problems, every imperfection. Running with my arms outstretched, calling His name, He will meet me just as I am. He will be, He is my best friend.

Victoria

Then Samuel took a stone and set it up between
Mizpah and Shen. He named it Ebenezer,
saying, "Thus far the Lord has helped us."

—*1 Samuel 7:12*, NIV

Jennie (three years old)
Summer 1975

GRANDMOM WARE GAVE me my baby doll Victoria. She is
so pretty. I love her beautiful white dress, and how her brown
hair is like mine even though her hair is painted on her head
and mine is soft and in pigtails. I have other dolls that sit
on my bed, but she is my favorite. Her eyes even open and
close. When she lies next to me on my bed, it looks like she
is sleeping.

Victoria isn't real, but she is my friend, kind of like Tabby
is my friend. I don't have a brother or a sister. Oh, I *wish* I

had a brother or a sister, but I don't, so me and Victoria like to be friends. She helps me when I don't feel well or when I am afraid. She comes with me every time I go see the doctor or when I have to go to the hospital. And I have to go to the hospital a *lot*. Sometimes, when we go to the hospital, the doctor has to take an x-ray of me. And guess what? He takes an x-ray of Victoria too! I get to see the x-ray of Victoria every time. The doctor shows me what she looks like on the inside. Deep inside, where no one else can see, she has a cry box and there's soft cotton around it. I like seeing her x-ray. It makes me feel like she will get better too. Then it's my turn to take an x-ray, and I get to hold Victoria the whole time. We go back together to my hospital room, and I squeeze her so tight. She is so *so* special to me. I love her!

The Umbrella of Protection

Submit to one another out of reverence for Christ.

—Ephesians 5:21, NIV

John

HELP ME TO be under your authority, Lord. I'm not telling you what to do. I'm asking you, God, put our family in order.

God had been teaching me powerful lessons out of Ephesians—what it truly meant to submit to His authority. Submission: a beautiful concept twisted into an ugly word. It is difficult to even say the word aloud without seeing people's shoulders visibly stiffen. But God's perfect intent for His loved ones is to nurture and protect them, which can only happen when His beloved willingly submit to His authority and design.

I thought of the protection of my strong umbrella. One rainy day, I had left it at home and found myself walking into a downpour without it. I was soaked to the skin within seconds, trails of cold water streaming over my face and dripping down to the ends of my fingers and onto the tops of my shoes. But had I been able to come under the protection of that curved fabric, I would have held firmly to that handle as I stepped into the rain, and I would have experienced protection from the harsh elements. There would be warmth, security, and safety.

God has created a perfect design for His imperfect people. He freely offers protection and loving guidance, but we must submit first to His authority.

As I learned more and more what it meant to give up control and submit to God, He was teaching me how to better lead my own family. How to lead with love and with a servant's heart. How to be willing to sacrifice everything for my beloveds, even when faced with difficult circumstances. *I don't understand why this is happening, but I'm coming under your authority. I want to have my relationship with you and the relationship with my wife right. I want to love her like you loved the church. Just put our home in order under your authority.*

My heart was filled to overflowing as I watched my family grow and thrive. I watched Cathie lovingly guide our daughter as she herself grew in Spirit and in truth. Our little girl was filled with joy as she learned to submit to our authority in the home. Our family's prayers together and individually were full of hope. There was a harmony and unity in our home that made the prayer covering all the more powerful.

We were multiple umbrellas covering each other lovingly and willingly under the authority of God, husband, and wife.

Together we intently prayed daily, and over a period of time, God started to give us little signs that He was working. It was a sense in our hearts that we were together in this. We cried out for the miraculous, and God kept telling us to keep going, keep working together. We thanked God for what He was doing. We couldn't see it yet, but we thanked Him anyway. Doctor reports always gave us a little element of hope. It kept us motivated—kept us together. We knew God was at work.

Because of this prayer covering, we felt more peace than anxiety. More hope and less fear. Were there fearful moments? Yes. Oh how my heart ached for the pain to be erased from the daily life of my little girl. But I knew that Jennie was feeling peace in her heart: a spiritual calm that could only be explained by our commitment to prayer.

Potty Prayers

I sought the Lord and He answered me;
He delivered me from all my fears.

—Psalm 34:4, NIV

Jennie (four years old)
Spring 1976

LORD, HELP ME please.

I'm a big girl, and I use the potty all by myself, but sometimes it hurts, so I'm going to ask God to help it not to hurt today. My mommy and daddy talk to God all the time. They pray by themselves, they pray together, and they pray with me. And it always makes me feel special when they are praying. They even told me that a *lot* of people pray for me. Can you believe that?

So when I'm scared, I like to pray too even when I'm all by myself, like right now here on my potty. I'm scared of the hurt, and I need help. I need a friend. My mommy told me that God wants to be my friend, so I like to ask Him to help me.

Last time I prayed, it still hurt. But you know what? My heart was still happy! God helps me to not be afraid and that makes me so happy inside.

Lord, please help it not to hurt.

No hurting today! Thank you, Lord! Thank you for hearing me. Thank you for helping me. Thank you for being my friend!

"The Dream"

> The great street of the city was of gold,
> as pure as transparent glass.
>
> —Revelation 21:21b, NIV

> After six days Jesus took with Him Peter, James
> and John the brother of James, and led them up
> a high mountain by themselves. There He was
> transfigured before them. His face shone like the
> sun, and His clothes became as white as the light.
>
> —Matthew 17:1–2, NIV

Jennie (four years old)
Spring 1976

IT'S DARK OUTSIDE now, so time for bed. Mommy just read the best story, and I wish, wish, *wish* that we could read just one more. All of those books on the shelf look so interesting! But mom says it's time for sleep, and I smile up at her as

I snuggle down under the cozy covers. I feel warm, safe, peaceful. We say prayers together, and I feel my eyes flutter closed as Mommy quietly tiptoed out, gently closing the door behind her. The room is dark, and I slip away into the darkness of restful sleep.

—⚒—

Gold everywhere! My eyes widen, and I can't believe what I am seeing. Gold pillars on the sides that are shining so bright that they look almost white, making my eyes squint just a little. The gold is so tall, so thick, bright, bold. I look down, and the road is made of gold too! There is a gate in front of me. A beautiful gate with shapes and patterns made out of the gold. So much gold! A king must live here!

I start to walk on the golden road, looking around at all of the shining beauty. My white dress matches Victoria's white dress, and I hold her tightly under my arm as I walk forward.

A tall gate is in front of me, so tall, and I am so very small. It opens, and I walk through. It is so beautiful and peaceful and there is a very bright light up ahead. The light makes my heart feel so happy, and I can't wait to get closer. When I am so close that the brightness surrounds me in my white dress, I lift my head and see a bright face. The light is so bright that I can't see anything except the face's shape, but I know that it is okay, and I'm not scared at all. In fact, I feel so happy looking at that face. And then I hear these gentle words, "Jennie, don't worry. I am going to take care of you. I am going to heal you after the baby is born."

I can't believe He knows my name! The voice is so kind, and I feel so much love in those words. I trust Him. I believe Him!

My eyes flutter open, and I see pretty streams of sunlight shining on the floor of my room. Victoria lies next to me on the bed. I still feel like I'm somehow floating in the light of the beautiful gold place. I gently push the covers out of the way and climb out of bed. I walk into the kitchen and tell Mommy, "I just had a dream."

After the Dream

So do not fear, for I am with you; be not dismayed, for
I am your God. I will strengthen you and help you;
I will uphold you with my righteous right hand.

—Isaiah 41:10, NIV

Cathie
Summer 1976

I WAS THINKING about, praying and believing daily for the
hand of Jesus to bring healing to my precious girl. There isn't
anything more important than trusting God for her health
and safety. I can remember the strong drive to protect her
from harm that I initially experienced after her birth when
we took her home for the first time. Amazed at how strong
this desire was, I knew He had put it inside of me. Months of
praying and not seeing changes in her condition turned into
a year. I continued teaching her scripture and filling her with

the hope that Jesus cared for her and He was with her. She took it all in and believed as any child would that her mommy was telling her the truth. The doubts would become strong, but I kept them inside and talked to Him as my friend.

Then I began to know.

In spite of the fact that physically she wasn't experiencing breakthroughs in her condition, I knew God was caring for her, and that He loved her more than I possibly could. It was a new concept for me. The lover of my soul embraced the little four-year-old love of my life with His strong arms and perfectly cradled her next to His heart. I had read about *perfect love*, even heard about it sung in an old song sometimes performed at weddings. But what did it really mean? Suddenly, what I had read in scripture came to life: "There is no fear in love, but perfect love casts out fear" (1 John 4:18a, esv). God brought peace and assurance of His presence and filled me with hope. The dream was confirmation of His care for her. She who had only seen Him in story books, heard about Him in scripture, and listened to her teachers talk about Him in preschool classes at church, began to experience His concern for her. And then the dream! She was with Him! He was with her now, and He had spoken. This brought us hope. She had seen and experienced His presence and heard His voice. When she awoke from her dream, I remember the wonder in her eyes and the delight in her voice. "Mommy, I was with Jesus. I saw Him, and He talked to me."

Trying to contain my own emotions as this wide-eyed little bundle of faith joyfully yet peacefully explained her encounter with the Living Lord of creation, I asked, "What did He say to you, Jennie?"

She looked into my eyes and said, "He said He is going to heal me, Mommy, without any surgery." Again, trying not to ask anything that would encourage her to tell me something I just wanted to hear, I said, "Did He say when this might happen?"

She gently said, "He told me He is going to heal me after my baby is born."

Speechless, I tried to take this all in. Finally, I remember saying, "Jennie, how wonderful, you got to be with Jesus, who loves you so very much! He is watching you and protecting you."

This was such a marvelous thing for me to experience! Now I am thinking, "How could this be, Jesus? How do you reveal yourself to four-year-olds? What is taking place here? Is this really you, Jesus? Do you really show up in this way? How will we know that this is a real encounter with You and not a figment of a four-year-old imagination?" I thought to myself, "If this is really Him, it will come to pass." So what next?

We scheduled more appointments with the doctor. The doctor would say, "I don't see any changes. The x-rays look the same. She isn't getting any better. The only thing keeping her from serious infection is the strong medication. She can't stay on that forever and will need surgery, most likely in the fall."

In the Spring, she turned four and we celebrated, as always, in a fun and special way, but my mind was racing. The baby Jennie was calling *her* baby that I was carrying would be around one-month-old, when Jennie would be wheeled into the operating room. How would I manage? What were we going to do? How could I breastfeed my newborn in a hospital while caring for Jennie after her major surgery? Living long hours and miles from family while my husband worked day and night as a student pastor produced a sense of fear and panic inside of me.

I sat in the doctor's examination room with my now four-year-old daughter. My hopes waning, but trying to *practice His presence* and remember He was with me and would sustain me through anything that would happen, I heard these words. "She will have major surgery. There is no other way for her to get well. It must happen."

Jennie heard those words, yet she remained incredibly peaceful, and I tried to act calmly while my thoughts were out of control. *What now, Lord? What do I say?* I looked at the doctor and said, "Are you sure? Isn't there any other way? We are having a new little baby, and I will need to care for my newborn and a small child having major surgery. I live very far away from family, and my husband is hardly ever home."

The doctor just looked at me and said, "Surgery will need to take place." I took Jennie by the hand and, at seven months pregnant, walked slowly down the ice-cold corridor of the medical center to the car.

Healed

But unto you who revere and worshipfully fear My name shall the Sun of Righteousness arise with healing in His wings and His beams, and you shall go forth and gambol like calves [released] from the stall and leap for joy.

—*Malachi 4:2,* AMPC

John
Winter 1976

FEAR. FATHERS AREN'T supposed to be scared. They are supposed to protect, provide, and wrap strong arms around trusting children. They are supposed to whisper gentle words of comfort while wiping away tears, "Don't be scared. Daddy's here."

But fear gripped my heart as I considered the inevitable upcoming surgery for my little Jennie. Months of doctor's visits had only confirmed what we feared most. Jennie would need to have surgery, and soon. The doctor said that there were no changes in her condition. The tubes and valves remained malformed, and the only thing that was keeping Jennie's body from suffering constant infections was the strong medication that she took every day. But she couldn't be on that medication forever. The doctors were adamant that the medicine was only a short-term solution. Taken longer than necessary, it could have other adverse effects on Jennie's body. Surgery was the only answer.

I would never forget the day that a doctor had described the surgery to us. He wanted us to know what it would entail so that we could "prepare ourselves emotionally."

"We're going to have to open her up from her spine to her belly button on one side and go in to fix those tubes," the doctor explained.

I didn't want to hear it. I couldn't imagine my precious girl having to be split open like that on a cold operating table. The doctor went on to say that after six months to a year, she would need to return to the operating room so that they could perform the same procedure on the other side of her little body.

Two major surgeries in one year. One little girl trusting in two scared parents.

How in the world can we do this? I thought to myself.

Jennie had already undergone several minor procedures—small incisions to open up an area for urine to pass through. Those had been traumatic for all of us. I was haunted by the vision of Jennie's tiny body, so pale, lying on that metal gurney, with Victoria at her side, being wheeled into the operating room as Cathie and I sat helplessly in the waiting room. A "minor surgery" that had seemed so major when it involved a bright-eyed, pigtailed preschooler. She was always so brave, grabbing the nurse's hand and following her to the table. I always wished that some of Jennie's courage could fill my own anxious heart as I held Cathie's hand and prayed with her during the procedure.

This, however, *this* was major surgery. The doctors were not sugarcoating anything. They wanted us to be prepared for what would need to happen.

On a cold December morning, I held Jennie's hand as we walked into the exam room. This was it. This was a presurgical appointment in which we would discuss a surgical plan. At our last visit, another x-ray had been taken, and the doctor would make his final surgery decisions based on what was happening in Jennie's body as evidenced by what could be seen in the glossy film. I prayed to myself, *Lord, if there is any way that this surgery can be avoided. Please."*

I sat down nervously next to Cathie in the sterile exam room and watched Jennie walk around, curious about everything she was seeing. As I had observed so many times before, there was a calm reserve in her. No agitation, no nervousness. Just the typical behavior of a four-year-old girl with her mommy and daddy. She knew she was safe.

The door opened, and in walked our doctor, followed by another young man in medical scrubs. We had been told when we checked in that there was an intern there working with our doctor, learning from him. Our doctor looked at us and said, "Well, I've asked this other guy to come in with me because this is one of those rare occasions that happens in my experience. Some people call it a miracle. I don't really understand it. I don't see any major changes, but somehow it's working. There's a flow there, and it's operating the way it should operate. I don't understand it, and I can't explain it. It just *is*. I don't know how it happened—"

Cathie jumped in, "Well I know how it happened!" She grabbed Jennie's hands, and the two of them started jumping up and down in exuberance, joy, disbelief, heart-bursting gratefulness. So many emotions filled that tiny exam room in that moment.

The doctor continued, "You'll still need to bring her back from time to time so that we can keep an eye on this because we can't tell you that this is a done deal. All I can tell you is that there is no need right now for surgery. It still doesn't look right, but it's functioning."

So there it was. The tubes were still not perfect, but they were functioning perfectly. Such a great reminder of the perfect work our Father does in and through our imperfect lives.

The doctors left the room, and I wrapped my arms around Cathie and Jennie. In the quietness of that little room, we paused to offer thanks for this miraculous healing.

Moments later, I found myself skipping down a hospital corridor, my faithful wife and my beautiful *healed* daughter skipping at my side.

New Life

> But now, this is what the Lord says—He
> who created you...He who formed you..."Do
> not fear, for I have redeemed you; I have
> summoned you by name; you are mine."
>
> —*Isaiah 43:1b*, NIV

Jennie
January 1979

A LITTLE MORE than two years had passed. I experienced a complete healing. What Jesus had said, He had done! For the first time, I was enjoying consistent health and wholeness. I was spending wonderful moments with my church family and fun with my dad's youth group. I loved this life. I watched and understood what it really meant to have a personal relationship with Jesus Christ. I had role models who patterned their lives after Jesus and had *fun* too! Crazy fun, yet had serious and meaningful moments with the Father. I watched that unfold every church meeting and youth group. I saw hundreds of teenagers sing and worship while dad played his guitar. It was making an impact.

On Sunday night, January 7, 1979, we were on our way home from Sunday night church. Dad was driving, mom was beside him, and my little sister sat next to me. I remember reaching forward and tapping my dad on the shoulder. I told my dad that the Lord had spoken to my heart. Jesus had said these words to me, "Jennie, I want you." I knew what that meant. It was time for me to give my heart to Jesus. My dad explained that we would go home and talk about it more.

Mom settled my two-year-old sister into bed and then joined dad and me in the living room. Dad explained how I could know Jesus. He and my mom wanted to be sure I understood what I was doing. It was such a sweet time. When I was ready to pray, dad led me. At 10:45 p.m. I prayed and gave my life to Jesus. Mom prepared bread and juice in the kitchen. We had communion together, the three of us. What a wonderful moment. I remember feeling so excited, so free! I belonged to Jesus! Finally, it was time for bed. My mom and dad tucked me in, and prayers were said. As my dad walked away and closed my bedroom door, I said to him, "Daddy, will Jesus ever leave my heart?"

In his most endearing yet confident way my dad said, "He will never leave you."

I felt so relieved! Such freedom! Those liberating words gave me great peace. I nestled in my bed, sure of my relationship with Jesus, then fell into a deep and restful sleep.

Part II

Jennifer

A STORY IS built on pain and triumph. To experience triumph, we must go through pain. We must face difficult times and sometimes the unbearable. Here, join me as I tell you the second half of my story. The deep longing, the disappointment, and what seemed to be a silent God, threw me into a turmoil I didn't understand. How could a loving and healing God allow me to experience this? What was His purpose and plan for it? I didn't know. There were no answers.

Floored

> "He was despised and rejected by mankind, a
> man of suffering, and familiar with pain."
>
> —*Isaiah 53:3*, NIV

2002

I SAT ON the cold tile floor. I reached down to tie my white Nike shoe, sporting a purple sports bra and black jogging shorts. It was time for my midmorning walk. My heart was thrilled and filled with excitement. I was six days late! As I sat there contemplating how I would tell my husband Matt that we were expecting again, I envisioned the way I had told him the first time. The bottle with jelly beans? The positive pregnancy test? No, this would be different. It had to be.

After Jake was born, we knew we wanted to have more children; however, we had been on a three-year roller-coaster of infertility. We had seen doctors and a specialist, and now it seemed like all of this was behind us. I was excited. Just the day before, I grabbed the brown cardboard box out of the closet full of maternity clothes I stashed away from 1998. I found the red adorable pantsuit my in-laws had given me along with a few others and decided they would be great to wear again even though it was 2002. I was prepared. I had it all planned out.

We visited the doctor a few weeks ago. I took medication, and the doctor ran tests. She said time would tell. I was doing everything the doctor instructed, and I prayed fervently, "Lord Jesus, please give us another baby. We know what you can do. We know you can!"

As I sat there ready to get up to walk, I felt a small cramp. *I've felt these before. This feels just like the other time when I was newly pregnant with our first*, I said to myself. Then another, a bit stronger than the last. The cramping became more intense, and my heart sank. The tears flowed, and I knew. It wasn't meant to be. Again, not this month. It was hard to take. We had wanted this for so long. We had tried everything. I sat on the floor paralyzed with grief. Through my tears, I said these words, "But God, we did what the doctor said. We have prayed so much for so long. We are following you the best way we know how. We are even parenting our child based on biblical truth. None of this makes sense!" In my anger, sorrow, and pain, I lay down on the floor sobbing, my body engulfed in deep sorrow. Intense emotional pain reached to the depth of my being and shook me. The three-year journey of disappointment imprisoned my soul. I could not escape. I had no way out. I cried out to God, hands raised, "God, please help me, please help me!"

I mustered up the strength to crawl over to my VHS player. My jogging outfit soaked with tears, I fumbled through my videotapes. At the bottom of the pile, I found it. A worship video I had watched and listened to over and over. It brought encouragement and strength in dark times. At the moment, I knew this videotape was all I had. I was grasping for anything that would bring relief. It was the only thing I knew to do to bring solace to my broken heart. I put the tape in the video player and listened. I had no voice. I was silenced. The words washed over me for a long time. Lifeless, I lay on the floor raw and empty. I had nothing to give God but suffering. I needed God to see me. I needed Him to share in my burden. I needed to be rescued. I needed Him.

The Truck

One thing I ask from the Lord, this only do I seek; that
I may dwell in the house of the Lord all the days of
my life, to gaze on the beauty of the Lord and to seek
Him in His temple. For in the day of trouble He will
keep me safe in His dwelling; He will hide me in the
shelter of His sacred tent and set me high upon a rock.

—*Psalm 27:4–5*, NIV

Fall 2002

IT WAS A morning like any other. It was a Saturday, and I
was busy with morning chores and minding a small child
amongst the laundry, bathroom cleaning and floor mopping.
Little hands were undoing all the tidying I had done, yet my
heart was so full of the gift of this little one God had given
to us. Pacifier half-tilted gripped in tiny lips, tousled brown
locks and pitter-patter feet followed me most everywhere. I

experienced such happiness and unexplained emptiness all in one.

We continued in our third year of trying to expand our family, and though we sought extensive medical advice, endured tests, medications and procedures, we remained a family of three.

How can this be, Lord? How can there be such happiness and emptiness at the same time? I felt guilty. I was perplexed and troubled that in the deepest part of me there was such a vast longing. These thoughts consumed me as I meditated on them and swiftly moved through the house on a schedule.

Saturdays were always busy days, but today added a particularly busy appointment. Our church worship team planned to meet at a recording studio for a recording session of a CD we would release a few months later. In anticipation for my afternoon, I continued to hurriedly clean and tidy, making sure my little family had what they needed for my afternoon away. The morning minutes marched on quickly as my morning rush fell into the lap of my afternoon. Trying to remember every detail, I hugged and kissed my husband and little one, opened my car door, got in, and tried to keep my speed in check. I was slightly behind schedule as I drove away to the studio. The drive was uneventful and plain, mostly just watching the dashboard clock, trying not to speed. Being a few minutes late was usually the norm for me as I maneuvered through motherhood. The studio was now in sight, and I drove up and parked, all the while talking to the

Lord about my life. I talked to Him about my emptiness and longing all in one.

The recording session was work. Many stops, starts, do-overs, pitch checks, and more. We stood in a circle for hours then sat on the floor during breaks. My mind spun with thoughts in-between, yet the music was a place of peace. Oh, to be in a room with friends, singing for hours, and not just music, but worship! How fortunate and blessed I was to do this kind of work! It brought me joy in a time when joy was not constant. Pain and longing for more children had been taken from me in that moment. For now, I experienced joy.

The five-hour recording session had come to an end. I hugged my girlfriends and said my good-byes. Strangely enough, I didn't want to leave that place. I knew beyond the doors what I would face: the stone cold reality of my situation. I wanted to stay within those walls of peace amongst the safety and comfort of friends. I didn't want to face my emotions alone, yet I knew I couldn't stay there. My small family awaited me.

In my reluctance, I pushed the glass door open and made my way to the car. My thoughts raced as I turned on the ignition, *Lord, what do you want from me? What more can I give you? My life is all I have!* As I drove through the back roads, I kept asking Him the questions over and over. By the time I reached the freeway, I was in a pleading state. I begged Him, *Please, Lord! Tell me what you want me to do. I'll do anything to get what I want! Please end this misery!*

He heard me and what happened next I had never experienced before. As I drove, a large white truck slowly merged in front of me. As I looked at the back of the truck, there was a scripture reference written in large words: Psalm 27:4–5. I wasn't familiar with the scripture, but I knew this *had* to be a promise from God for me! I mean, really! A scripture on the back of a truck? My car couldn't take me home fast enough. As I drove, I thought about all God was going to say to me through His Word. I was convinced that it would be a profound promise. There was hope! What did this mean?

My thoughts consumed me as I approached my house and parked. I walked inside, hugged and kissed my husband and son, then an hour later, in the quiet after bedtime routines, I sat down in the living room and opened my Bible to Psalm 27:4–5. The words read this way:

> One thing I ask from the Lord, this only do I seek, that I may dwell in the house of the Lord all the days of my life, to gaze on the beauty of the Lord and to seek Him in His temple...

Okay, Lord, I've read it. Is this it? Is this exactly what you want me to do? I was admittedly disappointed. This word I had received wasn't enough! There were no promises for me! There were no promises of a bigger family. That was what I wanted to find in the pages of that book! I was angry! *This is nothing, Lord! What do you mean by this? I'm supposed to gaze on your beauty and seek you in your temple? I'm supposed to dwell in the house of the Lord all the days of my life? Lord, I'm already doing that! What about telling me that I can have hope? What about giving me a promise? What about me?*

In my selfishness, I continued in this way with God, I didn't read on. I ignored verse 5. I was so put out by verse 4, I couldn't see past it. I was upset! How could this God whom I begged, petitioned, and pleaded with for answers, ask me to gaze on His beauty and to dwell in His house all the days of my life? I was ungrateful. I was very clear with Him. I had spoken my mind to the creator of the universe. There was no guessing about how I felt or the selfish heart I had given to Him. I stomped, kicked, I screamed, and then I gave up, *Okay, Lord, I'll do what you say. I'll gaze on your beauty, and I'll dwell in your house. I'll do it.*

With reluctance, I began to spend time with God. I worshipped. Minutes turned into an hour. As I sat quietly in my living room, I felt His presence. I gazed upon His beauty. And then I read on to verse 5. The words came to me like a rush of fresh water to my soul. This was the promise: "For in the day of trouble, He will keep me safe in His dwelling; He will hide me in the shelter of His sacred tent and set me high upon a rock."

God was doing what He had promised. He was lifting me, and the weight of heaviness began to lighten. He was setting me high on a rock. My redeemer, my friend, my help, and only deliverer had met me. He was there when I needed Him most!

Pool Cover

"For my thoughts are not your thoughts, neither are your ways my ways", declares the Lord. "As the heavens are higher than the earth, so are my ways higher than your ways and my thoughts than your thoughts."

—*Isaiah 55:8–9,* NIV

Summer 2003

IT WAS A beautiful Southern California summer morning. The sun was shining, and a work day ensued before us. The garage door was open, filled with things calling out to be done. We went in and out of the garage finding things to do and chores to complete. Anything to avoid what was in the backyard.

We had neglected the pool cover. It had disintegrated, and it was algae-infested and spider-ridden over the pool. Busy schedules had allowed the trash to invade the lovely space, and in many ways, the pool cover was a metaphor for us. We were a worn, disintegrated mess. We were dealing with raw emotions as we continued to struggle with infertility treatments and medications. Nothing worked, and we were spent. In our depletions, our communication suffered, and neither of us had much to give at all. We were two people desperate for answers. We were desperate for a silent God to show up somewhere, somehow.

As we continued about our day, the pool cover was left untouched, and words between us were at a minimum. I was trying to hold it all together, but I was screaming inside. I was screaming about my unanswered prayers and why a God who had shown up so miraculously before seemed to be deathly silent in a moment that was so desperate. I was a time bomb waiting to explode. The day moved on, and everything on the to-do list was checked off, except for the pool cover. Finally, the garage was empty of things to do. My husband had made his way to the backyard to pull off the filthy cover over to the side yard. He grabbed the recycle bin and brought two pairs of scissors with him. He handed a pair to me and said to start cutting the cover so that it would fit in the recycle bin. I watched him first, studying his hands to be sure I could manage. I'd never cut up a pool cover before.

As we cut in silence, we each found it somewhat therapeutic—so much pain and nothing to say. After what seemed like hours, my husband broke the silence with words, "Why are you cutting the cover that way? I told you to do it like this!" Usually, this kind of direct tone wouldn't bother me much, but this time, it was the wrong thing to say at the wrong time.

"I don't know why I am cutting the cover this way!" I screamed at the top of my lungs. Tears streamed down my face. I threw the pool cover and the scissors. "I don't know why anything is this way!" I was screaming so loudly I'm sure the neighbors heard. I had lost it in my own front yard. The tears and anger kept coming like rolling waves so fast. They enveloped and choked me as I gasped for air. I was at the height of what I thought was a spiritual betrayal. I was mourning the losses of my life, and there was nothing I could do. I was convinced that God had left me to suffer, and He wasn't going to send relief.

I stormed into the house and ran to the bathroom. Sobbing, I grabbed the vanity, the pain so deep as vomit welled up from my stomach, and I gagged it down. My husband left me there for a little while. He was wise. I was processing, and he was giving me space. Soon he peered in and met me in the bathroom.

"Why are you with me?" I screamed. "Why do you want me? I can't give you what you want! I can't give you more children! You could go find someone else who can give you what you want! Just leave me!"

"Jen!" he said, hands gently placed on my shoulders and eyes locked with mine. "I don't want anybody else. I want you! I don't want to have children with anyone else!"

"But, you could leave me and have what you want." I said softly.

"Jen, I have what I want. I want you. I'm not going anywhere."

Those words he spoke brought so much comfort to my soul. I fell limp in his arms and said, "I just don't understand what God is doing! Doesn't He see us? Doesn't He care?"

"Jen, I don't understand. But the one thing I do understand is this, His ways are not our ways, and His thoughts are not our thoughts. His ways are much higher than ours. We may not understand now, but we have to trust."

Looking up in His eyes I said, "I just don't get it! Why are we facing this? Why?"

"Jen, I don't know why. I don't know why," he said.

Then I let it all out. My husband embraced me, allowing me to release the pain I had carried for that day and the days before. I soaked his shirt with tears, and he held me tighter. In silence, we stood in the bathroom. God had met us, and this time through my husband. For a moment, I felt relief and at peace.

God Provides

Abraham answered, "God himself will provide
the lamb for the burnt offering, my son."
And the two of them went on together.

—Genesis 22:8, NIV

Fall 2004

IT WAS TIME for our annual trip to a large women's conference in Anaheim, CA. My mother-in-law and I made the trip once a year with our church to enjoy an inspiring, encouraging, and fun-filled weekend. Great teaching and worship awaited us. It was one of my favorite times of the year! It was something I needed.

I asked God specifically before the weekend to reveal something to me. Anything! I needed to know His thoughts about what I was going through. I was available and desperate to hear from Him. I sought after His heart. Little did I know what He was going to say to me. It was something I did not expect. It was raw, real and required something I wasn't sure I could do. Nonetheless, it occurred this way.

As usual, I arrived to conferences, church, and social events in a sad mood. Hoping no one would notice, I plastered a smile on my face and walked into rooms as brave as possible. All my life I was known as the "happy one." People even accused me of being fake because of my happiness, but truly that's how I was made. It was just a part of me. The disheartening thing was, for the first time in my life, I was experiencing sadness all the time. Yes, sadness came and went all the time; but this kind of sadness never went away. It would not relent! I honestly didn't know what to do with constant sadness, so I pretended. I continued to be "happy." I shared my emotions with dear friends and family, but for the most part, everything else was kept deep within my heart.

That day at the women's conference, I smiled. I engaged myself in worship and listened to amazing women teach about the goodness of God and His faithfulness. I listened to the teaching and enjoyed the worship, but I was sad inside. All day long, I had a silent conversation with God and told Him exactly how I was feeling. *God, I just don't know what you want. What can I give you so that you will give me another child?*

See what was happening? I had motives. My whole reason for reading God's Word and for prayer was to get what I wanted. I was bargaining with God. I was telling Him, "If you tell me what you want me to do, I'll do it, and then you can give me what I want!" That was the real deal I was making with Him. "Just tell me what you want, God! I'll do it! I won't question it! I'll do it! Anything!"

I repeated these words silently over and over to Him throughout the day of the conference. I was so consumed. I was completely focused on getting what I wanted: another child! I had plans! I had hopes! I had dreams! I wasn't asking for a million bucks! I was asking for a child, for heaven sakes! I begged Him. I pleaded with Him for hours. He wasn't speaking or revealing anything to me. He was silent.

The conference ended, and my mother-in-law and I drove home. It was late. Late enough that when I arrived home, I fell into bed quickly so that I would be ready to make the road trip back to the conference early the next day. Before I closed my eyes, I quietly said to God, "Just tell me what you want me to do!" Then, within minutes, I was asleep.

As I slept, the Lord revealed something to me that was shocking and true all in one. He showed me a picture of Abraham and Isaac. You know the story. The one where God asks Abraham to take his only son Isaac up to the mountain to lay him down on the altar as a sacrifice. That's what I saw: a precious boy, the object of Abraham's affections. The all-consuming precious Isaac. He was Abraham's whole world. A true gift. God was asking Abraham to be obedient even if it meant the death of his son Isaac. But that wasn't the end of it! In Abraham's complete obedience, God provided the lamb! God provided for Abraham in his obedience!

As the dream continued, God showed me a white lamb, a spotless one that emerged from the light-brown thicket. And in that moment, these were His words to me: "I am all you need. Lay down on the altar of sacrifice what is most important to you. Lay down your longing for another child. Do you trust me? I am your provision. I am all you need."

In silence, I opened my eyes and stared at the ceiling, my husband resting beside me. I was speechless. What do I say to that? I needed forgiveness. I had focused my motives and intentions so much on what I wanted that I had forgotten the dear and loving relationship of the Father. I had forgotten how to talk to Him just because that's what daughters and fathers do. I knew God understood why I was so consumed, and in His loving way, He used a powerful and unique story from His Word to show me how I had to change. I was putting too much emphasis on my longing, and I wasn't paying attention to the relationship I had with God. He was telling me to trust that He was my provision even if I didn't get what I wanted. He was enough!

Stunned, I continued to lie quietly, *I'm sorry, Lord. Please help me to trust you. I'm sorry I've forgotten to thank you for the blessings in my life. I'm sorry I allowed myself to get so wrapped up in my wants, even if my wants are good.*

Well, that was out of the way! I apologized to God, but I knew He wanted more from me, and it took a while. And then I did it. I spoke the words that were so painful to say, but I knew He wanted to hear, "I lay it down, Lord, on the altar. I trust you with the most precious desire I have. I give it to you. I trust you. You are enough for me. You are my provision."

Now I have to admit that in the very near moments to come, I repeatedly had to lay this desire down on the altar. I had to risk it, even to the death of my hopes and dreams for more children. I kept giving it to God. There were days I gave it to Him minute by minute, but I knew this was what I had to do. Jesus wanted all of me. He didn't just want my pleading. He wanted His daughter back! He wanted me to visit with Him like we used to do. He wanted me to talk to Him about everything, not just the one thing that consumed me. He knew my desire. I had made sure of that, and now it was my turn to lay it on the altar and let Him have it completely. Like Abraham, God was calling me to be obedient, and with His help, for that time, I was able to do it.

My Formula

In her deep anguish Hannah prayed to the Lord, weeping
bitterly. And she made a vow, saying, "Lord Almighty, if
you will only look on your servant's misery and remember
me, and not forget your servant but give her a son, then
I will give him to the Lord all the days of his life..."

—*1 Samuel 1:10–11*, NIV

Fall 2004

I HAD TRIED everything. Giving this desire to God, begging,
pleading, bargaining, and praying. Every day I poured out
my heart to God, asking Him to relieve the pain. He was
helping me, but that wasn't enough. I was receiving wonderful
promises from God's Word and finding comfort and relief in
small doses. The doses of relief, much like a soothing balm,
provided temporary healing when the pain was too much to
bear. It felt like a solid Band-Aid, a good one. The Band-Aid

would work for a while, and then an open wound of emotional pain would surface from deep within my heart. But I needed more! I wanted deliverance my way!

As I sat quietly in my living room with my Bible, tears streamed down my face. I was at my wit's end. I had allowed myself to succumb to despair and depression. In my desperation, I scrambled to do something that could possibly be the secret formula to fulfilling my desire for another child. As I sat, not praying at all, I had an idea! It was a perfect thought! Yes! I'll find Hannah's prayer in the Bible! I knew her story! She's the one who couldn't have any children. She prayed to the Lord, and He gave her a child! That's it! It had to work! "Okay, God," I said, "I've tried everything, and yes, you've told me to lay it down and to trust you, and yes, you've been faithful to show up, at times. So thank you for that. But I want more! I know you've told me that you are enough, and thank you for that too. I just have to try this! I'll pray Hannah's prayer exactly the way she did, and then like magic, I will have a child too! You did it for Hannah. Surely, you will do it for me!"

And so, in my selfishness and in a sort of hocus-pocus way, I was using God's Word to try to get what I wanted. I frankly didn't care about how God had met me time and time again. I was so wrapped up in my loss and pain. He knew it, and in my ignorance, He was so gracious and merciful. He let me explore in my childish ways and, I'm sure, lent an ear to this ill-motivated prayer.

"Here goes," I said. I glued my eyes to the Bible and spoke each word of Hannah's prayer to God. "Lord God Almighty, if you will only look on your servant's misery and remember me, and not forget your servant but *give* her a son, then I *will give* him to the LORD for all the days of his life."

I must have said this verse a hundred times! I made sure I said it exactly right! Surely, God would do this for me now. Can you believe it? I was so stubborn! Here God was making it abundantly clear that He was enough, and I wasn't accepting it or believing it! He wanted me to trust Him, that He would sustain me. He wanted me to understand that His Word would not be used as a magic book for my selfish gain! Oh, how deceived I was! I could not accept that Almighty God could fill this incredible void, and I wasn't giving Him the chance to do it! I was in so much pain that I allowed myself to spiral fast. I refused to let go! I refused to allow God to invade my heart and touch the darkest place! I was going to keep on begging, pleading, agonizing, and bargaining with Him until He gave me what I wanted! I wasn't going to accept anything else! After all, He had healed me physically once before so He just *had* to work the same way in my life again!

I stated Hannah's prayer one more time. Then I stopped. "All right, God. That should do it," I said. I closed my Bible and hoped for the best. After saying Hannah's prayer, there was complete silence. God didn't say anything to me. There were no answers, and there was no magic. Nothing happened. In days to come, I held on tightly to my desire, and even though I was "trying" to give it to God, I was failing miserably. I refused to let go. I held on to wanting more children with everything I had, and there was no relief. I would not trust. God remained silent for days, and we still remained a family of three.

Alone

Therefore I will not keep silent, I will
speak out in the anguish of my spirit, I will
complain in the bitterness of my soul.

—*Job 7:11*, NIV

Winter 2004

IT WAS AN ordinary day but a lonely one. I was busy getting
ready for church that Sunday morning. It had been a good
weekend. We met with friends, and our son enjoyed park days
and playdates. I had much to be thankful for. God had blessed
me, yet I chose not to recognize the blessing. My one prayer,
the one prayer that mattered most was not answered. My soul
felt empty and alone. Inside, I was an emotional wreck.

Our church service had begun. I tried to listen to the
sermon, but my mind was occupied with other things. Finally,
the service ended, and it was time to go home. We got up to

leave, and I managed to engage others in surface conversations and smiled the entire time. I didn't want to lose it in church! We walked out of the church building hand in hand with our son as our friends smiled and waved good-bye.

The drive home from church was the same each Sunday. We recapped the sermon and asked our son what he had learned in Sunday school. That Sunday, we talked about some of it, but not much. I wasn't in the mood.

We arrived home from church, had a quick lunch, and quiet rest time. Each of us went to our resting spots. Mine was on the couch in the living room. As I walked there, I took a deep breath and whispered these words to God, "I'm feeling so alone. I am in so much pain. I need someone or something to help me! Why won't you give me what I want? Why won't you give me another child? Why? Why won't you answer my prayer? Why have you chosen to be silent? I can't do this! Don't you understand? I can't do this!" Tears of agony and pleading continued. I was unpacking another wave of grievous emotions. I was a child in desperate need for God to give me something He wasn't willing to give, and I couldn't understand.

"God, please send the pastor's wife to pray with and encourage me. If you are hearing me, you will be that specific, she will show up! Surely you will do that! Prove yourself this way to me!" I begged some more, and the tears streamed freely as I sat upright in the living room chair. The begging intensified. "God, please send her, please! I need someone to help me!" The emotional pain was grueling. "God, please, please!" I kept begging, and in my anger I wailed these words. "You healed my body! When I was little, you told me you would do it, and you did! Now you are choosing not to heal me! You have left me here! What am I supposed to do with that? Tell me! What am I supposed to do?"

Sobbing, I gripped the couch pillow and held it tightly. In the other room, my husband kept his distance. He was tired of the pain. He tried to help, but my need was greater than what he could give. He was emotionally spent, and I was convinced that we needed someone who could come and help. Someone who would pray. Someone who would listen. I felt isolated and alone. Who would come? Who would come to my rescue? Who would help carry this burden? No one. No one would come to see me that day. I kept looking out the window in hopes that someone, anyone had heard from God—even if it wasn't the pastor's wife—anyone! I'm quite sure that the Lord in all His mercy would have sent someone had that been the best for me.

But He chose otherwise. He had another plan. God chose not to send a visitor to me. He wanted to send himself, but I wasn't receiving Him. He wanted to reach into my heart and comfort me. He wanted me to trust Him, and I could not. He wanted to take my loneliness, and I wanted to hold on. I was so angry and wanted things my way. I could not understand His plans or His ways.

The Gift

For it is by grace you have been saved through faith
and this is not from yourselves, it is the gift of God.

—*Ephesians 2:8*, NIV

Spring 2005

SADNESS WAS THE norm for me. I expected it, and by this
time, I embraced it. It seemed that every woman was pregnant
or having babies! I'm sure it really wasn't happening that way.
But with sensitive emotions, it sure seemed like it! The smell
of babies and the touch of babies! Oh, how I longed for just
one more! Just. One. More.

It was Saturday afternoon. The sun was shining, and the
beautiful Southern California spring weather allowed us
to be outside. The outdoors was my five-year-old's favorite
place! Prying him off a little league field or from the bottom
of a tackle pile in the front yard was commonplace. He was

precious. A beautiful and vibrant miracle all in one. Jesus had given him to us, and the doctors could not believe we had him. Early tests showed a condition that nearly made it impossible for me to carry a child. This little boy was our miracle! If you ask him, he will tell you he is a miracle. I love that! A miracle indeed!

But even in the reality of our miracle, my thoughts and emotions remained clouded. As I looked at our son, I couldn't understand why I didn't feel like he was enough! He should be all we need. I felt guilty for wanting God to do the miraculous again, but I just couldn't escape it! I quietly studied my five-year-old son as he played in our backyard. He ran, jumped, and embraced the day. I watched him well, and then I dared to ask for more, "God, thank you for our son. He is a miracle, and I am grateful. But I need more! I need something, a gift, a sign, something that lets me know you are there."

In the past, I had asked for so many things, and in His goodness He gave them to me. He gave me peace, dreams, and promises from His Word. He had made himself known. I should have been satisfied. God didn't have to do anything for me. He didn't have to grant my request. He didn't have to give me a gift to prove himself, but He did. In His infinite mercy and grace, God gave me a wonderful gift. A gift that mattered for eternity!

Later, my husband, son, and I came inside, dusted off and finished our day. It was clear that God's goodness and faithfulness were right before our eyes. What a sweet little boy! Quietly I said, "Thank you, God, for allowing me to be a mother. Thank you!" That evening as we went through bedtime routines, our son finally climbed into bed. His red-white-and-blue "All Star" PJs were wrinkled up around his chubby little legs. My husband and I sat with him on the edge of his bed. Then what came from his tiny voice was beautiful and pure: "Mommy, Daddy, I want to become a Christian. I want to ask Jesus to come into my heart."

This was the gift God gave me! God was prompting our son to follow Jesus! It was a far greater gift than I could have ever imagined. I was astounded and speechless. What amazing love and grace from our Heavenly Father! During that sweet time in our son's room, my husband explained God's plan of salvation. Little eyes looked and little ears carefully listened as my husband explained words in terms our boy could understand. After my husband shared God's plan, our son knew and was convinced it was time to give his heart to Jesus. That night, Jake's life would never be the same. Prayerfully, all three of us huddled on the small twin bed. We held hands and bowed our heads. Then my husband Matt led our son through a simple and meaningful prayer. It was a tender and sacred moment. A moment forever etched in our hearts.

Oh how the presence and power of God filled that place! God had met us! Our son was receiving an incredible gift! The free gift of Jesus! *Thank you, Lord, for this answered prayer! Thank you for giving me the gift of watching our son commit his life and his ways to you! How could I ask for more?* The hour was late. We hugged our boy and tucked him in. Our hearts were full. God had answered my prayer in a profound and incredible way. The sadness was lifted once again.

Wholeness

He said to her, "Daughter, your faith has healed you.
Go in peace and be freed from your suffering"

—Mark 5:34, NIV

Fall 2005

IT HAD BEEN years now. So many doctor visits, tests, medication and more tests. Our son reached the age of six, and the reality of having one child sank into a low place in my heart. It was difficult to accept it. I asked God for more children, and He wasn't willing to give them to me. I couldn't understand. I was confused and depressed, *Why, God? Why are you choosing to take the dream of more children from me? You know what this is like for me. I'm so sad. Please don't ask me to go through this anymore. Please heal my body and please let me have more children.*

There was no answer to my continued prayer. I began to believe lies about myself. Certainly, I had failed as a mother, I am not a good enough wife, and God doesn't trust me. That must be why. There were no other logical reasons. I was emotionally broken, and the sadness was unbearable. I spent so much time crying out to God. My prayers went up, hit the ceiling, and came back down. I wanted this so badly, and He was saying no. It was hard to take.

One particular day, I was sitting in the living room while my son played quietly in his playroom. I stared off in the distance in a daze as the sun shown on my face through opaque curtains. The warmth of the sun was good, and in the quiet, I closed my eyes and said these words to God, "Please, God, don't you remember me? I'm the little girl you talked to years ago. I'm the one you healed. You took the suffering away. You helped me. Why won't you help me now and heal my broken body?"

As I continued to pray, God gently reminded me about the woman with the condition of blood. The Bible tells us in Mark 5, about a woman who had a bleeding condition for twelve years. She spent all of her money on treatments from many doctors, and nothing helped. In fact, her condition got worse! She was considered unclean by Jewish law. That means she was exiled from the temple, and anyone she came in contact with was considered unclean as well. But that didn't stop this woman! She was courageous and determined. She wanted to be healed! She took whatever measures necessary to get to Jesus. When she heard about Jesus and what He could do, she had incredible faith! She was desperate for a miracle! She came up behind Jesus in the crowd and wanted to reach down to touch the hem of His garment, "If I can just touch His clothes, I will be healed!" (Mark 5:27–28). The story continues, and she does just that! She touched Jesus's garment and was healed immediately! Jesus felt the healing power leave His body, and He asked who touched Him. The woman stepped forward and told Jesus that she touched Him. Then He said, "Daughter, your faith has healed you. Go in peace and be freed from your suffering" (Mark 5:34).

"Okay, Lord," I said as I walked into our son's playroom and watched him play. I continued my conversation with God. "Thank you for the reminder about this story in the Bible. What do you want to teach me?"

As I was talking to God, I reached down to the ground. I picked up our son's toy and heard these words, "Rise daughter, your faith has made you whole." Still knees to the ground, I looked up and saw my smiling boy's face in front of me. As I stood up, I had an idea in my mind of what I thought that meant! I had suffered for so many years. We had spent a good portion of time and resources to accomplish what we wanted, and nothing helped. I knew Jesus could heal me. "Okay, God. This must mean you are going to physically heal me! You said my faith has made me whole, and I believe that! Thank you."

I got up off the floor and continued to help our son clean up the playroom. I had a new hope. Another moment of relief from the pain that consumed me. My faith had made me whole! Yes! I took these words literally. I'd like to say I was right. I'd like to say that I was physically healed. But it didn't work that way. God had another plan. That moment would be a segue of an extraordinary encounter that would change my life. Forever.

The Net

I waited patiently for the Lord; He turned to me and heard my cry. He lifted me out of the slimy pit, out of the mud and mire; He set my feet on a rock and gave me a firm place to stand. He put a new song in my mouth, a hymn of praise to our God. Many will see and fear the Lord and put their trust in Him.

—Psalm 40:1–3, NIV

Winter 2005

IT WAS A low day. A day like no other. In the past, I experienced pain, suffering, despair, and grief. But this was different. A wave of depression came over me. I reached a low that was unfamiliar. It was lower than the lowest of days. Walls caved in, and the darkness took over. Numbness surrounded my body. I could not escape. My resilience and willingness to cry out to God were gone. I had done that so many times before.

I had repeatedly asked Him to remove the deep pain and agony from me. I had fought for so long. I was tired, and I was done.

In the other room, our son played quietly. The remembrance of what I did that day was vague. There was no memory of the everyday responsibilities of a wife and mother. I'm not sure I was functioning. In order not to disturb our son, I went into the living room and lay on the couch. I lay there for a long time in a trance. As I lay there, tears trickled warmly down my cheeks as the salty liquid reached my lips in a sharp sting. I didn't have anything left to say. The pain was too strong. I had to go. I needed to leave. I had to get out. I gave up. In silence, by myself, I began to say these words to God, "Let me go. I don't want to do this anymore. I can't. Please let me go. Please. Let. Me. Go." I kept saying these words to God, and tears flowed freely. I asked God to take me.

I closed my eyes and rolled from the couch to the floor. I laid face down, tears soaked the off-white carpet. Then I saw my body fall into a deep dark pit. I fell deeper and deeper. In anger, I gritted my teeth and said, "Let me go! Just let me go!" That's what I wanted. That's how I thought I could fix things. I didn't want to live with pain. I couldn't bear it. It was too much. I had to have a way out. I sobbed and begged and then silence. Lying there, I heard these words, *No, Jen. I won't let you go. I won't let you go.* Each time I asked Him to release me from my life, He answered, *No. I won't let you go.* And each time, a greater peace came over me.

As I fell deeper still into the dark pit, I saw a white net in my peripheral. The net lay gently under my body. It gathered me up like a soft white hammock. It cradled me and rocked me back and forth, and He repeated the words, "I won't let you go, Jen. I won't let you go." I'm not sure how long I "lay" in the net. Minutes, hours? It's unknown. Nonetheless, I experienced a new level and a new place with God. I experienced a miracle. I opened my eyes, still face down on the carpet. My tears dried, I crawled over to the couch, grabbed the side and lifted myself up. As I did, I realized I wasn't the same. The depression lifted. The despair was gone. I had no more emotional pain. I had been restored! Yes, the sadness of not having more children was there, but the emotional death that entangled me finally released its grip. Contentment consumed my heart. A new attitude and gratefulness for my family and for God invaded my darkest place. I was completely new! Jesus took my brokenness and made me whole. I was delivered! All glory to God!

Hope

Therefore, since we have been justified through faith,
we have peace with God through our Lord Jesus Christ,
through whom we have gained access by faith into
this grace in which we now stand. And we boast in
the hope of the glory of God. Not only so, but we also
glory in our sufferings, because we know that suffering
produces perseverance; perseverance, character; and
character, hope. And hope does not put us to shame,
because God's love has been poured out into our hearts
through the Holy Spirit, who has been given to us.

—*Romans 5:1–5*, NIV

Winter 2007

I DON'T THINK we could have made it through our next
obstacle without the miracle I had experienced that dark day
back in 2005. We wanted more children, and our son wanted
a brother or a sister. He kept asking us about it and included

his request to God during night-time prayer. It was difficult to hear our son ask for a sibling and for us to not have an answer as to why we could not give him one.

My husband and I were emotionally drained from all the medications and tests. We knew we were ready to release this part of our life forever. It was after my emotional healing that I trusted God and gave it completely to Him. I believe God in His goodness allowed me to do that. The strength He gave and the joy He traded for my pain made the difference.

In our struggles, we decided that adoption would be the next logical step. It was a new thought that excited us to some extent. I say it that way because during the beginning stages, my husband and I had a terrible time seeing eye to eye on how all of it would work. It puzzled me because I thought that naturally this would be our next step. However, it wasn't that easy. There were countless conversations and doubts that would surround us, not usually at the same time. One of us would be "onboard," ready to jump in whole-heartedly while the other waded in the sea of uncertainty. The frustration of total agreement to whatever would lie ahead continued to linger, yet we pushed through the beginning process of adoption. We attended classes, gathered information, talked to adoptive parents, listened to testimonies, and enjoyed seminars. We talked with our son about the possibilities, and he seemed to be happy with it all.

We moved forward. There still was some unrest, but we knew that this had to be a part of God's plan. After all, He does say that as believers we are responsible to look after widows and orphans (James 1:27). So we pressed on. Our disagreements and questions mounted. We continued to submit paperwork and meet deadlines. We kept close contact with our agency, and we worked to be sure all our documentation was up-to-date and correct. We managed the legwork and asked God for direction.

The days of getting close to seeing a photo and a possible match for our family drew near. We were excited and scared. We had received a call from our agency that the country we chose to adopt from was ready for us to take the next steps. It was Christmas time, and we were excited about this special gift! We planned for the match and talked about what this little person would be like as a member of our family.

Then we waited. Days turned into weeks, and weeks into months. We had lost steady contact with the agency but received word through e-mails that the country of which we had chosen to adopt from was cautiously considering "closing its doors" to new adoptive parents. We had hoped and prayed that it wouldn't happen, but we were strong. We had a new fight and faith in us for whatever would happen.

Later, we received a call from the adoption agency informing us that the country was officially closing its doors. Our hearts were broken. We couldn't understand. The agency offered neighboring countries, and at the time, we declined. We just had to stop. We asked God to give us a clear direction. In our request, we realized that it was time to completely rest. We gave it entirely to God.

In the process, we knew that God gives hope in all things. The trials we faced were not in vain, and God used each part to build, mold, and shape our hearts. It's good to know that God continues to write our story. He is working out His plan. We trust day-by-day that, even though our son is our only child, God will take care of him and us, no matter what. God's plans are perfect. I know that full well. I have seen and witnessed His healing, His grace, His incredible love, and His deliverance that marked my heart and saved my life. I can't deny His healing or who He is or His power. He is relevant, relational, and real. He knows my name, and He knows yours too. His love reaches farther and wider than we can imagine. He is all we need. He comforts in our losses, fills our voids, and soothes our pain, if we allow it. He carries us in our darkest hour and brings hope to the hopeless. He binds up the broken-hearted and heals our wounds. He sets the captive free. He calls us for His purposes and predestines our steps. He stands in the gap, intercedes on our behalf, and fights for us against the wiles of the enemy. He is our defender. He is our friend. He is our rock on which we stand. He provides; He knows what's best. He understands. He is the creator and giver of all good things. He is all in all. He is everything.

Part III

Devotional Studies

The Phone Call Study 1

Let the peace of Christ rule in your hearts
since as members of one body you were
called to peace. And be thankful.

—Colossians 3:15, NIV

1. Reflect on Colossians 3:15. Now, rewrite it in your own words.
2. Think of a time you were facing an important life circumstance and describe your thoughts and feelings.
3. How might the truths stated in Colossians 3:15 have been applied to that circumstance or to a circumstance you are facing right now?
4. Is the Holy Spirit saying anything to you now about what steps to take? If so, write it down.

The Cure for Anxiety Study 2

Therefore I tell you, do not worry about your life,
what you will eat or drink; or about your body,
what you will wear. Is not life more than food,
and the body more than clothes? Can anyone of
you by worrying add a single hour to your life?

—*Matthew 6:25, 27*NIV

1. Read chapter 6 of the gospel of Matthew. Let God's Word penetrate your heart and mind.
2. What are you facing that seems overwhelming? How do the truths mentioned in Matthew 6 apply to what you're facing?
3. Quiet your heart and ask God to speak to you from Matthew 6. Write down any thoughts that come to your mind.
4. What is God saying to you about your relationship with Him? Record any insights.
5. Say a prayer in your own words, thanking God for speaking to you and caring for you.

Labor and Delivery Study 3

Hear my voice when I call, Lord; be
merciful to me and answer me.

—*Psalm 27:7,* NIV

1. Read all of Psalm 27 and record as many themes as you can from this passage.

2. Choose one theme that stands out and relates to you personally. Write it down.

3. Read verse 4. What is the "one thing" God is asking us to seek in verse 4? Why do you believe this is important for you?

4. Do you believe God hears you when you call to Him? Why or why not?

5. Read Jeremiah 29:11–13 and write down what the Holy Spirit says to you.

Delivery Room Study 4

Come unto to me all ye that labour and are
heavy laden, and I will give you rest.

—*Matthew 11:28*, KJV

1. Read several versions of Matthew 11:28 (AMP, MSG, NIV, and others). Let God's word penetrate your heart and mind. What is Jesus telling you to do in Matthew 11:28?

2. Name a struggle with which you are dealing.

3. How do the words of Jesus apply to this struggle in your personal life?

4. Read Matthew 11:28–30. Be quiet before the Lord and ask Him to speak to you from the scripture. Write

down any thoughts that come to your mind. What changes in your personal life do you need to make in order to experience the rest Jesus is describing in these verses?

5. Read Isaiah 40:28–31 (KJV, AMP, MSG, NIV). Meditate on the truths in this chapter. What do the verses in this chapter say about God?

6. Write a list of the characteristics of God mentioned in Isaiah 40:28–31. Read this list aloud to the Lord, thanking Him for His beautiful qualities.

My Girl, God's Gift Study 5

Children are a gift from the Lord; they are a reward from Him. Children born to a young man are like arrows in a warrior's hands.

—*Psalm 127:3–4*, NLT

1. What does God say about children in Psalm 127:3–4?
2. How do you think God sees you as His child?
3. Read Psalm 139:1–18. List some ways you are a gift to your father God.
4. What is the Holy Spirit saying to you about your personal value to God?

First Year Study 6

Trust in the Lord with all your heart and lean not
on your own understanding; in all your ways submit
to Him, and He will make your paths straight.

—Proverbs 3:5–6, NIV

Read chapter 3 of the book of Proverbs. Let God's word
penetrate your heart and mind.

1. List several themes that seem obvious to you in this
    chapter.
2. What predominant theme applies to you?
3. How do verses 5 and 6 relate to the predominant
    theme you are seeing?
4. Are you facing a major situation now that requires a
    decision? Based on God's word in Proverbs 3, what do
    you believe the Holy Spirit is telling you to do?
5. Read the following passages and write down what
    God is saying to you about your relationship with
    Him: Isaiah 11:2–3, Phil. 4:4–9, Psalm 27:7–8, Isaiah
    30:19–21.
6. What step is God asking you to take regarding your
    relationship with Him?

Florida Study 7

Hear my cry, O God; attend unto my prayer. From
the end of the earth will I cry unto thee, when
my heart is overwhelmed: lead me to the rock
that is higher than I. For thou hast been a shelter
for me, and a strong tower from the enemy.

—Psalm 61:1–3, KJV

1. Read Psalm 61:1–3 and underline key words in this passage.
2. Think about a time when you felt overwhelmed. Write a brief description of what that time was like. How did you react?
3. What are some ways that God can be a shelter of protection for you?
4. How is God described in Proverbs 18:10 (NIV)? What kind of assurance does this provide for you?

News Study 8

But seek first His kingdom and His righteousness, and
all these things will be given to you as well. Therefore
do not worry about tomorrow, for tomorrow will worry
about itself. Each day has enough trouble of its own.

—Matthew 6:33–34, NIV

Meditate on Matthew 6:33–34. Write down the main point of this verse.

1. Recall a time when you received news that was shocking or frightening. Briefly describe this event.
2. Do you ever face recurring distractions that cause you to worry or lose focus on God? If so, explain briefly.
3. How does the main point of Matthew 6:33–34 help bring focus to your situation?
4. Read Psalm 62. Based on this psalm, what steps will you take now to relinquish your worries to God?

Pink Study 9

Love must be sincere. Hate what is evil; cling to what is good. Be devoted to one another in love. Honor one another above yourselves. Never be lacking in zeal, but keep your spiritual fervor, serving the Lord. Be joyful in hope, patient in affliction, faithful in prayer. Share with the Lord's people who are in need. Practice hospitality.

—*Romans 12:9–13*, NIV

According to Romans 12:9–13, read and list action steps for demonstrating love.

1. When you walked through a difficult time, did you do this alone or in community? What was it like for you?

2. Have you received love from others during a difficult time? Explain briefly.

3. What are some ways you will demonstrate love to someone in need?

4. Ask God to bring to your mind someone who needs to receive love. Write down their name, and what you will do to help them. Consider doing this in community with others.

Melodies, Memory Verses, and Medicine Study 10

A cheerful heart is good medicine, but a
crushed spirit dries up the bones.

—*Proverbs 17:22,* NIV

1. Think about a time when you experienced a "crushed" or defeated spirit. How did you respond? Explain briefly.

2. Where does your cheerful attitude come from? What kinds of things do you do to make yourself feel happy?

3. The Bible says a cheerful heart is like good medicine. What does this mean to you?

4. Ask God to show you a specific area where you need a cheerful attitude. Ask Him to give you the strength to change your attitude. Write down what God says to you.

Songs and Stripes Study 11

But He was pierced for our transgressions, He
was crushed for our iniquities; the punishment
that brought us peace was on Him, and by
His wounds (stripes KJV) we are healed.

—Isaiah 53:5, NIV

Read Isaiah 53. This chapter is a description of Jesus. List the
things mentioned that He experienced on the cross.

1. Why was Jesus willing to suffer like this on the cross
   for you? What was His greatest passion?
2. How does it make you feel when you think about the
   suffering Jesus was willing to endure for you?
3. In what ways does this passage speak to you about His
   love? What does this mean to you?
4. When realizing the magnitude of Jesus's love for you,
   how does this impact your relationship with Him?

Questioning and Comfort Study 12

Praise be to the God and Father of our Lord Jesus
Christ, the Father of compassion and the God of
all comfort, who comforts us in all our troubles, so
that we can comfort those in any trouble with the
comfort we ourselves have received from God.

—2 Corinthians 1:3–4, NIV

> Perfume and incense bring joy to the
> heart, and the pleasantness of a friend
> springs from their heartfelt advice.
>
> —*Proverbs 27:9*, NIV

Read and reflect on 2 Corinthians 1:3–4.

1. Describe a difficult time in your life. Did you experience God's compassion or comfort?
2. Do you know someone in your life who is suffering? How might you be a source of compassion or comfort to them? Ask God to direct you.
3. Reflect on Proverbs 27:9. Think of a significant friendship in your life. How might you be a blessing and comfort to your friend? How might your friend be a blessing and comfort to you?

Tabby Study 13

> A friend loves at all times, and a brother
> is born for a time of adversity.
>
> —*Proverbs 17:17*, NIV

1. Describe the qualities of a loving friend.
2. How has a friend demonstrated love to you?
3. What will you do to show love to a friend?

4. Read John 15:12–17. Explain the friendship Jesus wants to have with you. How does Jesus want you to respond to His invitation of friendship?

Friends (Disabilities and Discoveries) Study 14

Christ arrives right on time to make this happen. He didn't, and doesn't, wait for us to get ready. He presented himself for the sacrificial death when we were far too weak and rebellious to do anything to get ourselves ready. And even if we hadn't been so weak, we wouldn't have known what to do anyway. We can understand someone dying for a person worth dying for, and we can understand how someone good and noble could inspire us to selfless sacrifice. But God put His love on the line for us by offering His Son in sacrificial death while we were of no use whatever to Him.

—*Romans 5:6–8*, MSG

1. What does the Holy Spirit want us to understand about Jesus in Romans 5:6–8?
2. Based on this passage, how does Jesus want us to come to Him?
3. Why would Jesus die for us before we deserved it? What was His purpose?
4. Stop now and thank God for His unconditional love for you.

Victoria Study 15

Then Samuel took a stone and set it up between
Mizpah and Shen. He named it Ebenezer,
saying, "Thus far the Lord has helped us."

—*1 Samuel 7:12,* NIV

Read 1 Samuel 7.

1. Samuel and the nation of Israel experienced a great victory over the armies of the Philistines. Before the victory, the Israelites were terrified and asked Samuel for help. What was Samuel's response to their request (see verse 7)?

2. Describe a conflict or battle in your life.

3. What significant event do you remember occurring in your conflict/battle when God intervened and provided a victory?

4. According to 1 Samuel 7:12, to remember God's victory in the battle, "Samuel took a stone and set it up." This would serve as a reminder of the way God helped the nation of Israel. Is there something tangible you have that reminds you of God's faithfulness during your conflict/battle? If so, what is it? If not, ask God to bring something to mind, for example, a special plaque with a scripture or a photograph.

The Umbrella of Protection Study 16

Submit to one another out of reverence for Christ.

—Ephesians 5:21, NIV

Write down your personal definition of submission.

1. Why do you think of submission, in either a positive or negative way?
2. In relationships at home, at church, and at the workplace, how might you demonstrate an attitude of submission?
3. According to Ephesians 5:21, what should be your motive for submission?
4. Consider one step you will take to exhibit submission to a significant person in your life.

Potty Prayers Study 17

I sought the Lord and He answered me;
He delivered me from all my fears.

—Psalm 34:4, NIV

1. Recall a time in your life when you experienced uncertainty that produced fear. Describe your reaction to this uncertain time.
2. What does Psalm 34:4 say to do when faced with fear?

3. What does God say He will do when you seek Him?

4. Take a moment and write a prayer to God asking Him for His help when facing fear.

The Dream Study 18

The great street of the city was of gold,
as pure as transparent glass.

—Revelation 21:21b, NIV

After six days Jesus took with Him Peter, James
and John the brother of James, and led them up
a high mountain by themselves. There He was
transfigured before them. His face shown like the
sun, and His clothes became as white as the light.

—Matthew 17:1–2, NIV

1. How does Revelation 21:21 describe this part of heaven? What does this tell you about the nature of God?

2. Read Matthew 17:1–9 (NIV). Why did Jesus take His disciples up a high mountain? What was Jesus trying to show them?

3. Ask God to reveal himself to you in a personal way.

4. When God reveals himself, how will you respond?

After the Dream Study 19

So do not fear, for I am with you; do not be dismayed,
for I am your God. I will strengthen you and help you;
I will uphold you with my righteous right hand.

—Isaiah 41:10, NIV

Has there ever been a time when you were afraid, asked God for help, and you didn't see anything happen?

1. Are you trusting God now for something without seeing results? Briefly explain.
2. Based on Isaiah 41:10, what does God promise to do when you are afraid?
3. What do you think He wants you to do in the midst of your dilemma?
4. Do you have assurance of God's hope and love? If yes, press in to Him through prayer and His Word. Receive His strength. If no, ask a Christian friend or a pastor to pray with you and help you.

Healed Study 20

But unto you who revere and worshipfully fear My name
shall the Sun of Righteousness arise with healing in His
wings and His beams, and you shall go forth and gambol
like calves [released] from the stall and leap for joy.

—Malachi 4:2, AMPC

Read Malachi 4:2 and explain what you think it means to fear the name of the Lord.

1. According to this passage, who does the Sun of Righteousness represent?
2. How might Jesus bring healing into your life today? Briefly explain.
3. Are there unique ways God reveals himself when you need spiritual, emotional, or physical healing? If so, describe your experience.
4. Consider sharing your experience with a friend.

New Life Study 21

"Do not fear, for I have redeemed you; I have summoned you by your name; you are mine."

—*Isaiah 43:1b*, NIV

Quiet your heart and think about the words in Isaiah 43:1b.

1. Express in your own words how you see Jesus' loving heart in this passage.
2. Recall the time when Jesus became more than a concept to you. Describe your experience.

If you have not encountered Jesus personally, do you believe He loves you and cares about you? Read Romans 10:9–10 (NIV). If you declare with your mouth, "Jesus is Lord" and believe in your heart that God raised Him from the dead, you will be saved. For it is with your heart that you believe and are justified, and it is with your mouth that you profess your faith and are saved.

Now, consider praying and telling Jesus you need Him. If you just made the decision to confess Jesus as Lord of your life, tell one friend or a pastor at a local church about your decision.

3. What are some steps you can take to deepen your relationship with Jesus? Consider asking a friend to partner with you and provide accountability as you take next steps.

4. If you are not involved in a local church, ask your friend to help you find one in your community.

Floored Study 22

He was despised and rejected by mankind, a
man of suffering, and familiar with pain.

—*Isaiah 53:3a*, NIV

How is Jesus described in Isaiah 53:3a?

1. What specific words in this passage show that Jesus understands your pain?

2. Read John 19:1–7 (NIV). Describe in your own words how Jesus suffered.

3. Think about how the sufferings of Jesus apply to your personal suffering.

4. Because He is familiar with pain, ask Jesus to enter into your pain and carry you through it.

The Truck Study 23

One thing I ask from the Lord, this only do I seek; that I may dwell in the house of the Lord all the days of my life, to gaze on the beauty of the Lord and to seek Him in His temple. For in the day of trouble He will keep me safe in His dwelling; He will hide me in the shelter of His sacred tent and set me high upon a rock.

—Psalm 27:4–5, NIV

According to Psalm 27:4–5, explain what the psalmist instructs you to do.

1. When you focus on the Lord, what does He promise He will do?

2. Reflect on a time when your situation was out of control. Describe your thoughts and feelings.

3. Sit quietly and ask the Lord to tell you what to do to bring focus to your situation. When you think He shows you what to do, and it lines up with the Word of God and character of God, take action.

4. Pray and give your situation completely to the Lord.

Pool Cover Study 24

"For my thoughts are not your thoughts, neither are
your ways my ways", declares the Lord. "As the heavens
are higher than the earth, so are my ways higher than
your ways and my thoughts than your thoughts."

—*Isaiah 55:8–9*, NIV

Write Isaiah 55:8–9 in your own words. What stands out to
you in this passage?

1. How are the Lord's ways and thoughts higher than yours?
2. Name something noble that you wanted the Lord to do for you but He was not willing to do it.
3. Read John 11:1–44.
4. What did you learn about the Lord God and His ways when reading the story in John 11:1–44?

God Provides Study 25

Abraham answered, "God himself will provide
the lamb for the burnt offering, my son."
And the two of them went on together.

—*Genesis 22:8*, NIV

Read Genesis 22:1–13.

1. What did God ask Abraham to do? How did Abraham respond? What struggles do you think he had?

2. Look at verse 7, what did Isaac ask his father?

3. Even though Abraham could not see God's immediate provision, he had to release complete control and trust God. Think about an area of your life where you need to trust God. Release control and trust He will provide for you.

My Formula Study 26

> In her deep anguish Hannah prayed to the Lord, weeping bitterly. And she made a vow, saying, "Lord Almighty, if you will only look on your servant's misery and remember me, and not forget your servant but give her a son, then I will give him to the Lord for all the days of his life..."
>
> —*1 Samuel 1:10–11*, NIV

In 1 Samuel 1:10–11, Hannah was desperate for God to answer her prayer. Recall a time when you were desperate for God's intervention.

1. In Hannah's misery, she asked God to look at her and remember her. Record a situation where you needed God to notice you and understand you.

2. What was your motive for asking God to answer your prayer? Do you believe your motive was right? Why or why not?

3. Read 2 Corinthians 12:7–10(NIV). What happened to Paul? What was God's response to Paul?

4. What does God want to teach you about Himself and His relationship with you?

Alone Study 27

Therefore I will not keep silent; I will speak out in the anguish of my spirit, I will complain in the bitterness of my soul.

—Job 7:11, NIV

Based on Job 7:11 (NIV), write down in your own words what Job said to God in his time of crisis.

1. When you are in crisis, what do you do? Explain briefly.
2. God wants you to be real and transparent with Him. He desires an intimate relationship with you. Tell Him exactly how you feel or have felt when you are in crisis.
3. God wants to love you in your crisis. He wants to talk to you. Take time and listen. Stay in His presence until you believe you have heard God. Write down one thing you believe He is saying to you about His love.
4. Accept what you believe God is showing you about His love. If you have questions about what you have heard, tell a trusted mature Christian.

The Gift Study28

> For it is by grace you have been saved, through faith
> and this is not from yourselves,it is the gift of God.
>
> —*Ephesians 2:8,* NIV

Based on Ephesians 2:8, what is God's gift to you? What do you need to do to receive it?

1. An outward expression of our love for God is to do good works. We are saved by grace in order to do good works (see Ephesians 2:9–10). What type of work does God want you to do?
2. How can you represent God as a volunteer in your work, in your church, or in your community?
3. How can you represent God in your home?
4. God has given you the gift of salvation. What will you give Him in return?

Wholeness Study 29

> He said to her, "Daughter, your faith has healed you.
> Go in peace and be freed from your suffering."
>
> —*Mark 5:34,* NIV

Read Mark 5:24–34. Write a summary of the story from these verses.

1. What did the woman in this story want from Jesus?

2. In order to receive what she wanted, what did the woman believe she needed to do?

3. All of us have suffered physical and emotional pain. Sometimes it can last for years or a lifetime. Explain your experience with physical and or emotional pain. Did you feel Jesus caring for you during that time? If yes, describe Jesus's care. If no, stop now and ask Him to reveal His care for you.

4. Realize that Jesus wants to take the broken and empty pieces of your physical and/or emotional pain. He knows the kind of healing you need. Ask Him and receive what He gives you.

The Net Study 30

I waited patiently for the Lord; He turned to me and heard my cry. He lifted me out of the slimy pit, out of the mud and mire; He set my feet on a rock and gave me a firm place to stand. He put a new song in my mouth, a hymn of praise to our God. Many will see and fear the Lord and put their trust in Him.

—Psalm 40:1–3, NIV

1. Think of a time when you were at a very low point. Perhaps that time is now. Briefly describe the situation from the past or present.

2. Based on Psalm 40:1–3, how does God show up in desperate situations?

3. Has God revealed himself in the midst of your life circumstance? If so, explain. If you are still waiting, keep asking. God is able.

4. When God helps you, express your thanks to him. Celebrate!

5. Tell others about what He has done for you.

Hope Study 31

Therefore, since we have been justified through faith,
we have peace with God through our Lord Jesus Christ,
through whom we have gained access by faith into
this grace in which we now stand. And we boast in
the hope of the glory of God. Not only so, but we also
glory in our sufferings, because we know that suffering
produces perseverance; perseverance, character; and
character, hope. And hope does not put us to shame,
because God's love has been poured out into our hearts
through the Holy Spirit, who has been given to us.

—Romans 5:1–5, NIV

1. What does Romans 5:1–5 say about the relationship between hope and suffering?

2. How do you glory in your sufferings? Explain.

CPSIA information can be obtained
at www.ICGtesting.com
Printed in the USA
FSOW02n1520030916
24555FS

9 781682 707883

John and Catherine Ware

3. Because of the work of the Holy Spirit, God's love has been poured out into your heart. How does this truth give you hope? What will be your response to the hope God has graciously given you?

Matthew, Jennifer and Jacob Gentry
(Photos by Tobey Leier)